# PET
# STORIES

*Thank you for using your library*

D1334003

**Look out for all of these enchanting story collections**
by *Enid Blyton*

# Enid Blyton

# PET STORIES

Illustrations by Mark Beech

# HODDER CHILDREN'S BOOKS

This collection first published in Great Britain in 2021
by Hodder & Stoughton

1 3 5 7 9 10 8 6 4 2

Enid Blyton® and Enid Blyton's signature are registered trade marks
of Hodder & Stoughton Limited
Text © 2021 Hodder & Stoughton Limited
Cover and interior illustrations by Mark Beech. Illustrations © 2021
Hodder & Stoughton Limited

A CIP catalogue record for this book is available from the British Library.

ISBN 978 1 444 95430 2

Typeset by Avon DataSet Ltd, Arden Court, Alcester, Warwickshire

Printed and bound in Great Britain by Clays Ltd, Elcograf S.p.A.

The paper and board used in this book are made from
wood from responsible sources.

Hodder Children's Books
An imprint of Hachette Children's Group
Part of Hodder & Stoughton
Carmelite House
50 Victoria Embankment
London EC4Y 0DZ

An Hachette UK Company
www.hachette.co.uk
www.hachettechildrens.co.uk

# Contents

The Mysterious
Thief

# The Mysterious Thief

EVERY MORNING the milkman left a bottle of milk on the doorstep. Billy-Bob used to take it in sometimes, and it felt very cold and slippery. He was careful not to drop it.

'Belinda, look at the cream on the top of the milk,' he said each time he brought the bottle in. 'We can have it on our porridge!'

It was fun to watch their mother pour the milk into a jug, and then on to their porridge. Billy-Bob and Belinda liked to swish it round their plates. Wags, their dog, liked to lick out the top of the milk bottle, if only he could find it somewhere within reach!

One morning, when Billy-Bob went out to get the bottle of milk from the doorstep whatever do you think he saw? Why, the milk bottle was upset, the top was off and the milk was gone!

'Oh, Mummy!' cried Billy-Bob, rushing indoors. 'Mummy! Someone has stolen our milk! Look, the bottle is empty. We've no milk for breakfast.'

'Oh, what a pity,' said his mother, vexed. 'Now we shall have to use the little drop I had left over last night. I hope it isn't sour.'

'It isn't,' said Billy-Bob when he tasted it. 'Mummy, who do you suppose stole our milk? Wasn't it a horrid thing to do?'

'A very horrid thing,' said Mother. 'I can't imagine who it was.'

'Perhaps it was that little boy who makes faces at us at the bottom of the road,' said Belinda.

'Oh, you mustn't say things like that,' said Mother. 'He may pull silly faces, but I am quite sure he wouldn't steal somebody's milk.'

'Well, Mummy, who could it be?' said Belinda, stirring her porridge around.

'I don't know,' said Mother. 'Belinda, don't stir your porridge round any more; you'll make it giddy! Eat it up!'

So Belinda ate her porridge up, and Billy-Bob ate his, and nobody said any more about the stolen milk.

But, would you believe it, when Billy-Bob went to get the bottle of milk the next morning the milk was gone again! Yes, it really was! The bottle was once more lying on its side, the top was off and the milk was gone. There were just a few drops on the step, but that was all.

'Mummy, the milk's been stolen again!' yelled Billy-Bob, rushing indoors with the empty bottle.

'Billy-Bob, don't run with a glass bottle,' said Mother. 'You know that it is a very dangerous thing to do. Oh, dear – so the milk is gone again. Well, I haven't a single drop this morning, so you will have

5

to go and ask Mrs White next door if she can lend us some.'

Billy-Bob went to ask Mrs White, and she gave him a jugful because her milk had not been stolen, so she had plenty. Billy-Bob carried it carefully home without spilling a drop. He thought and thought about their own milk, but he simply couldn't imagine who had stolen it.

'Mummy, let's put Wags in the hall to sleep tonight,' he said. 'Then if anyone comes in the early morning after the milkman has left the milk, Wags will hear them and bark. Then they will be frightened and will go away.'

'That's a good idea, Billy-Bob,' said Mother. 'We will put Wags's basket there, and he shall sleep just by the door.'

So that night Mother put Wags's basket in the hall by the front door. Wags was surprised. He stood looking up at Mother, wagging his tail as if to say, 'All right, mistress, I will sleep here – but it seems to be a funny thing to do!'

Mother knew what Wags said. She could always read the language his tail spoke! 'It's all right, Wags,' she said, patting him. 'I just want you to sleep here for a few nights, and then if any bad person comes creeping up the path to steal our milk in the morning, you will hear them and bark!'

'Woof!' said Wags, wagging his tail. He jumped into his basket and lay down with his long ears drooping over the edge. He was on guard!

Now the next morning, at about a quarter past seven, Wags heard something. He awoke and sat up in his basket. Someone was scrabbling and scraping on the front doorstep. It was the milk thief! Wags jumped out of his basket and ran to the door. He scraped at it with his feet, barking loudly.

Billy-Bob woke up in a hurry. 'Wags is barking at the milk thief!' he cried to Belinda, who had woken up too. 'Quick, come to the window and see who it is!'

Billy-Bob and Belinda ran to the window and

looked out, but, do you know, they couldn't see anyone at all! Nobody went down the path in a hurry! Nobody ran across the garden! It was most mysterious.

'Perhaps it wasn't the robber,' said Billy-Bob. But, you know, it was! Because when Father went downstairs and undid the door there was the milk bottle knocked over again, and the milk gone!

'Well, really, this is too bad,' said Father. 'I shall tell our policeman about it. We can't get up early in the morning and watch over our milk every day. It is silly. The policeman will soon find out who is the thief.'

So Father went to see Mr Plod the policeman. He wrote down a great many things in his notebook and looked very serious.

'I haven't heard of anyone else having their milk stolen,' he said. 'It's very strange, sir, that it's just your milk! I'll keep a watch tomorrow. Do you mind if I hide behind that thick lilac bush in your garden?'

Billy-Bob and Belinda were most excited to think that Mr Plod was going to hide in their garden. They went and looked at the lilac bush and wondered if Mr Plod could really hide there. He was such a big man. Billy-Bob got into the bush and pretended to be Mr Plod. It was great fun playing policemen all that day.

Wags didn't sleep in the hall that night. He slept in his usual place in the kitchen. Mr Plod said it would be better not to have him near the door in case he barked too soon and frightened the thief away.

Well, Mr Plod got behind the lilac bush just after the milkman had left the milk. He couldn't see the front doorstep from the bush, but he could quite well see if anyone came up the path or crept round the house. He hid there and waited. He waited and he waited. Nobody came. Nobody even went down the street. When it was seven o'clock Mr Plod came out from behind the lilac bush and looked up at Father's bedroom window.

Father opened the window and looked out. 'Seen anybody?' he said.

'Not a single person!' said the policeman. 'I think the thief must have known I was hiding here this morning.'

Billy-Bob ran down to get the milk for his mother, but, dear, dear me, when he opened the front door there was the milk bottle on its side again, and all the milk gone!

Billy-Bob stared as if he couldn't believe his eyes. Really, it was very, very mysterious. How could the milk have been stolen when Mr Plod was hiding behind the lilac bush?

'Mr Plod, Daddy, Mummy, the milk has been stolen again!' shouted Billy-Bob. And then what a to-do there was! Mr Plod vowed he hadn't been to sleep in the lilac bush, and hadn't seen anyone at all. Wags barked. Billy-Bob told Belinda at the top of his voice all about it.

'Well, sir, I'm very sorry I couldn't see what happened to the milk,' said Mr Plod, looking quite hot and bothered. 'I'm afraid I can't hide again tomorrow morning because I'm doing something in the next village. But I'll come again on Friday and try.'

'Come and have a hot cup of tea,' said Mother. 'It must have been cold hiding out there so early in the morning.'

So Mr Plod had a hot cup of tea and he said it made him feel better. Then he got on his bicycle and rode away.

'Belinda,' said Billy-Bob that afternoon in an excited voice. 'I've an idea. What about me hiding and watching for the thief? If only I can wake up early enough, I could actually squeeze into the lilac bush!'

'Oh, yes, Billy-Bob, do!' squeaked Belinda. 'Let me come too!'

'No, Belinda,' said Billy-Bob. 'Mummy wouldn't like you to do that. You are too little. Besides, it was my idea. I want to do it.'

Billy-Bob didn't say a word to his mother about his idea, not a word! He was just a bit afraid she might think *he* was too little!

'I do hope I wake up early enough in the morning, Belinda,' he said when they were going to bed that night. 'Do you think I shall?'

'Oh, yes, I expect so,' said Belinda. 'Just say you want to wake up at seven o'clock, and perhaps you will.'

So as he went to sleep that night Billy-Bob whispered over and over to himself. 'I want to wake up at seven o'clock! I want to wake up at seven o'clock!'

And, do you know, when the hall clock was striking seven Billy-Bob awoke! Wasn't that clever of him? He sat up and listened to the clock striking. And then he heard the milkman coming up the path, he heard the thud of the bottle being put on the doorstep and the milkman going away again. Good!

Billy-Bob dressed very quickly indeed, but he only did up just a few buttons. He put on his coat and crept downstairs. Belinda was fast asleep. Nobody else was awake either. Billy-Bob had the whole house to himself. He let himself out of the back door. He ran to the lilac bush. He peeped first to see if the milk bottle was on the doorstep, and it was standing up, quite full.

Billy-Bob hid himself in the bush and waited for the mysterious thief. He waited and he waited, just as Mr Plod had done. But he heard no footsteps down the road at all.

Suddenly he heard something else! It was the sound of the milk bottle being tipped over, and yet Billy-Bob had seen no one going up the path to the front door at all! Still, the thief was there. Billy-Bob heard the sound of the milk gushing out! He jumped out of the bush. He ran bravely to the front door, crying, 'I've got you, I've got you!'

And then he saw the thief! Whoever do you think it was? Guess! It was their hedgehog, the one that Belinda had found at the bottom of the garden!

Would you believe it? He had come every morning to the doorstep, slyly tipped over the bottle, pushed off the top and then lapped up all the milk that ran out! Oh, you bad hedgehog – whoever would have thought it was you?

Billy-Bob stared and stared. There was the prickly hedgehog lapping up the milk and making a great noise as he did it! He didn't even stop when Billy-Bob came up to him. He knew Billy-Bob all right; Billy-Bob wouldn't hurt him! Why, he had often had saucers of food from Billy-Bob.

Billy-Bob ran round the house and in at the back door. 'Mummy! Daddy!' he shouted, running up the stairs. 'I've found the milk thief! It's our hedgehog! He tipped the bottle over, got off the top and then drank the milk!'

Well! His mother and father couldn't help laughing. So that was the mysterious thief after all! Just their own naughty hedgehog! Whatever would Mr Plod say when he heard? He would laugh to think he had hidden in the lilac bush to catch a hedgehog!

'You're a clever fellow, Billy-Bob!' said Father. 'You found out the thief when nobody else could! Well done!'

'Daddy, how are we going to stop the hedgehog from stealing our milk each morning?' asked Belinda.

'Oh, ask Billy-Bob that,' said her father. 'He's very clever; if he can find the thief, he can stop the stealing. What shall we do about it, Billy-Bob?'

'We'll ask the milkman to leave the bottle on the windowsill!' said Billy-Bob at once. Wasn't that a good idea of his? You see, the hedgehog couldn't climb up there!

So now the milk bottle is left on the windowsill, and it is quite safe there each morning. But the hedgehog is not forgotten; he gets a saucer of milk each day. Billy-Bob and Belinda give it to him. He's a lucky fellow, isn't he?

# The Rabbit With a Gold Tail

# The Rabbit With a Gold Tail

'I DO wish we could have a bicycle,' sighed Peter.

'So do I,' said John, his twin. 'But you haven't got enough money, have you, Mummy?'

'No, I haven't,' answered Mummy, 'and I'm afraid I shan't have enough to buy you a bicycle for ever so long.'

'Oh, dear, what a pity!' said the twins. 'We would so love one.'

'Well,' said Mummy, stopping her ironing for a minute, 'I've been wondering if you might perhaps earn some money yourselves to buy a bicycle.'

'Oh, how?' cried Peter, excited.

'Well, you know Snow-white, your big fluffy rabbit?' began Mummy.

'Yes, go on!' cried the twins.

'There is going to be a big rabbit show for the most beautiful rabbits round about our county,' went on Mummy, 'and I think perhaps if you fed and looked after Snow-white as well as you can, he might, perhaps, win a prize for you at the show.'

'Oh, and we could buy a bicycle then!' cried the twins joyfully.

'Yes,' said Mummy, 'but you mustn't hope too much! He's a lovely rabbit, but there may be lots at the show even lovelier than he is.'

Peter and John quite made up their minds that Snow-white should win the prize, and they went to tell him all about it. He looked at them and listened. He couldn't talk, but he seemed to understand.

'Isn't Snow-white getting nice and fat!' said Peter, three days afterwards.

'Yes,' said John, who was feeding him with lettuce

leaves. 'I think his fur is growing longer too.'

'It's only a week now before the show,' whispered Peter to Snow-white. 'Do see if you can grow lovelier every day. We shall be awfully proud of you if you win the prize.'

The days went by until the day before the show came. Peter and John were very excited, and kept going to visit Snow-white.

That night, when both little boys were asleep there came a tapping at the window. Peter and John woke up and listened.

'Let me in, let me in,' called a little voice. 'I want to ask you something.'

Peter ran across and opened the window. In flew a little fairy dressed in blue and silver.

'Oh, please,' she said in a very out-of-breath voice. 'Oh, please, will you lend us Snow-white for a little while?'

'Why, what *do* you mean?' asked John, astonished.

'Well, you see,' explained the fairy, 'the fairy

queen is going to visit her cousin, the prince of Dreamland, tonight, and she is travelling in her best carriage drawn by four beautiful white rabbits.'

'Like Snow-white?' asked John.

'Yes,' said the fairy, 'and one of them has got a thorn in its foot and can't go on. So the queen thought you would lend us Snow-white instead.'

'Oh, dear! I don't think we can,' answered John. 'You see, he's going to a show tomorrow, and we really can't spare him.'

'Well, I can't promise that he will be back in time,' said the fairy, 'but we'll do our very best. *Do* let us have him, because the queen is really quite upset.'

'All right, you can have him, can't she, John?' said Peter generously. 'If he doesn't get back in time, never mind, we'll have to do without him, though we *did* want him to win the prize.'

'Oh, thank you very much,' cried the fairy, flying out of the window. 'You won't mind if I turn his tail gold, will you, to match the other three rabbits?'

'Not a bit,' said John, feeling that a gold tail would make Snow-white look really quite exciting.

Next morning, when the twins went to Snow-white's cage he wasn't anywhere to be seen.

'Oh, dear,' sighed John. 'Snow-white isn't back from Dreamland after all.'

'And we shan't be able to take him to the show,' said Peter tearfully, 'but, never mind, I expect he was a great help to the queen.'

At that moment there was a floppety noise behind them. They turned around to see what it was.

'Why, here's dear old Snow-white back again!' cried John joyfully.

'And, John, look at his lovely gold bobtail!' exclaimed Peter.

Sure enough, Snow-white had a most lovely gold tail, and it certainly suited him beautifully.

'You're just in time for the show,' said Peter, picking him up. 'Come along, we'll take you.'

So Snow-white was taken to the show and put in

one of a row of little cages, where there were many other beautiful rabbits.

The judges found it very difficult to choose the most beautiful rabbit from among so many. When they came to Snow-white they stopped and said, 'Yes, this rabbit is very beautiful, but there's nothing extra special about him to make us give him first prize.'

'Oh, but there is,' cried Peter. 'Turn round, Snow-white, and show your gold tail!'

'What a wonderful thing!' cried the judges. 'However did he come to have a gold tail? Oh, we must certainly give him the first prize. He is quite beautiful, and most extraordinary.'

Snow-white was very pleased, and so were the twins, for the first prize was quite a lot of money.

'We'll buy a beautiful new cage for Snow-white,' said Peter to Mummy, 'and then we'll buy a bicycle with the rest, won't we, John?'

'Yes, let's,' answered John, 'and I say, Peter, wasn't

it a good thing we lent Snow-white to the fairy queen last night?'

'Yes, rather, because it was his gold fairy tail that won the prize!' laughed Peter.

# The Glittering Diamond

# The Glittering Diamond

ONE DAY Sandy found something in the grass.

'Ho!' he said. 'Look at this lovely glittering thing! It's a diamond, I'm sure! I'll have it made into a necklace for the mistress!'

He fetched Patabang, and she looked at it.

'Purr!' she said. 'That's a lovely diamond surely! It will look beautiful round the mistress's neck. Let's show it to Bimbo.'

So they fetched Bimbo, and he patted it with his paw.

'Mew!' he said. 'What a lovely thing! It feels so cold to my paw! Won't the mistress be pleased with it? Let's get Dion and show him.'

So they fetched Dion, and he sniffed at it.

'Woof!' he said. 'So that's a diamond, you say? Well, the mistress *will* be pleased with us! I've heard that diamonds are very valuable. Look! There's Bubbles, the kitten that lives with me. Let's show her.'

So they called Bubbles, and she came running over the grass to see the glittering diamond.

'Miaow!' she said, and brushed it with her whiskers. 'What a pretty thing! The mistress will be very grand when she wears *that*! Let's get Thomas the tortoise and show him too.'

So Thomas was fetched, and he touched the diamond with his little brown nose.

'Ooh!' he said. 'Isn't it cold? Won't the mistress feel chilly with that round her neck?'

'Don't be foolish!' said everyone. 'Nobody minds how cold a necklace is so long as it is beautiful!'

Then the pigeons fluttered down to have a look, and Bill tried to take it into his beak.

'*Rookity-coo!*' he said when it slipped out into the grass again. 'Isn't it slippery? My, what a beautiful glittering thing! The mistress *will* be surprised!'

'Oh, you naughty bird, you've bitten it smaller!' cried everyone. And, sure enough, it did look much smaller than when Sandy first saw it.

'Here comes Bobs!' cried Pat. 'He'll tell us how to get it made into a necklace for the mistress. Hie, Bobs, come here and see what we've found!'

Bobs scampered up – and, as soon as he saw that diamond glittering in the grass, he put out his tongue, gulped it into his mouth and swallowed it whole!

'Oh, you've swallowed our diamond!' shouted all the pets angrily. But Bobs sat down and laughed woofily.

'That was a piece of ice that the fishmonger dropped!' he said. 'Ooh, it *was* good to feel it slipping down my throat on this hot day. Thank you so much for finding it for me!'

Then he ran off to tell the mistress the joke.

'What kind pets I have!' she said. 'Fancy wanting to make me a diamond necklace out of a piece of ice! I'll give you all an extra-good tea today!' And so she did!

Twelve Silver Cups

# Twelve Silver Cups

JEFFERY WAS a splendid runner, and at his school sports he always won all the running prizes. His father and mother felt very proud when he went up to get the silver cups that were the reward for the best runner.

'Really, Jeffery,' said his mother, 'I shall have to have a special little cupboard made for you to keep your silver cups in! When you have twelve I will get you one.'

Jeffery already had eleven. So that year when he again won the prize for running he had his twelfth silver cup. How pleased he was!

'Now you'll have to get me that special cupboard

you promised,' he said to his mother.

'I certainly will,' she said. And in a week's time a nice oak cupboard came, with a glass door in front. There were two big shelves inside, and Jeffery proudly arranged his cups on the top one.

'Plenty of room for more cups!' said his mother, smiling at him. 'Don't they look lovely, Jeffery?'

Jeffery was proud of his cupboard. His mother showed it to people when they came to tea, and Jeffery liked to see people looking at it and hear them say how nice the cups were.

And then what do you think happened one night to those twelve silver cups? A burglar got into the house and stole them all! He hadn't time to take anything else because Spot the dog began to bark. Daddy woke up and heard a noise and tore downstairs – just in time to see a dark figure running down the garden.

Daddy switched on the light and saw that Jeffery's cups were gone. He ran into the garden, but the man had disappeared. So Daddy rang up the police.

But nobody seemed to be able to get back those cups. Jeffery was very unhappy, because they were his and he had been proud of them. It had taken him years to win them, and now he would have to begin all over again to fill his oak cupboard.

The policeman took a lot of notes and asked a great many questions. But he didn't catch the thief, though he said he felt sure he knew who it was.

'But I've gone into his house and looked all around while I've been questioning him, and I can't see the cups anywhere,' said the policeman. 'Maybe he's hidden them somewhere and will go and get them when the fuss has died down!'

Two weeks went by and nothing was heard of the twelve silver cups. Then another bit of bad luck came to Jeffery. He lost his tortoise!

He had had Slowcoach, his tortoise, for six years, and was fond of the quaint old creature. Slowcoach would let Jeffery tickle him under the chin, and would always poke his head out when Jeffery whistled a special whistle. Now he was gone!

'Oh, Mother, wherever do you think he can be?' said Jeffery. 'I've hunted over every bit of the garden.'

'He must have escaped into someone else's garden,' said Mother. 'You know how tortoises wander, Jeff.'

'But the wire between our garden and the next garden is quite all right,' said Jeffery. 'I've looked at it.'

'What about the wire at the end of the garden?' said Mother. 'That's not so strong.'

Jeffery went to look at it, and he looked very carefully indeed. Mother was right! The wire was not so strong there, and Spot had scraped at it and bent it back in one place so that he might get into the big ploughed field at the back.

'I guess that's where old Slowcoach got out!' said Jeffery to himself. 'Bother! He may be anywhere in that enormous field. Well, he's my pet and I'd better look for him.'

It was a cold day, and there was frost in the wind.

Jeffery buttoned up his coat, climbed over the fence and went into the big field. He simply didn't know where to begin to look for his tortoise.

'His brown shell is so like the earth that I don't believe I'd see him if he was right under my nose!' said the boy. 'Hie, Spot! Come and help me! Find Slowcoach! Maybe your nose will find what my eyes can't!'

Spot squeezed through the hole in the wire and danced over the field, yelping. He sniffed here and there, and then he and Jeffery both saw the same thing! In the middle of the field a piece of earth flew up into the air – and then another!

Jeffery ran over the furrows – and when he got to the place he laughed.

'It's old Slowcoach burying himself for the winter!' he said. 'What a long way you've walked over the field, Slowcoach!'

'Woof!' said Spot, and danced round the tortoise. There was nothing much to be seen of him except one hind leg, for he was now half buried.

Jeffery pulled Slowcoach gently out of the soil.

'Slowcoach, you have your own box of moss and bracken at home in the shed,' he said. 'That's where you sleep for the winter – not in a damp, cold field where you might be hoed up! Come along!'

Spot went to the hole and sniffed there. Then he began to scrape excitedly at the earth, and in a few moments Jeffery was spattered from head to foot with flying soil.

'Stop, Spot, stop!' he yelled. 'Are you thinking of burying yourself for the winter too? You're not a tortoise! Don't be silly!'

But Spot wouldn't stop. He went on and on digging – and then a strange thing happened. He pulled hard at a dirty brown rope and yelped loudly.

Jeffery put the tortoise down and helped Spot. He pulled at the rope – and a sack came slowly up from the earth. Something inside it clinked.

Jeffery undid the rope and looked inside the

little sack. And in it were his twelve silver cups! Yes, the thief had hurriedly buried them in the middle of the field, meaning to return for them when it was safe. There they all were in the dirty sack, very dull and tarnished, and with scratches here and there – but safe!

With Slowcoach in one hand, the sack over his shoulder and Spot yelping round his feet excitedly, Jeffery rushed home.

'Mother! Mother!' he yelled. 'I've found my twelve silver cups! At least, Slowcoach really found them, and Spot dug them up – but I've got them, I've got them, I've got them!'

He *was* so pleased, and so was his mother. Now she has cleaned them beautifully, and Jeffery has stood them all neatly on the top shelf of his cupboard.

'Slowcoach shall have a nice new box to go to sleep in this winter,' said Jeffery. 'And Spot shall have a new collar! I *am* pleased to have my cups back, Mother! I do wonder if the thief will know.'

The thief didn't know. He went digging in the field for the cups two nights later – and the policeman caught him. He won't go stealing twelve silver cups again!

Granny's Kittens

# Granny's Kittens

'DAISY, PUT on your hat and go to Granny's,' said Mummy. 'She has some nice homemade sweets for my sale of work, and I told her you would fetch them.'

'Oh, yes, Mummy – I'll go now,' said Daisy, pleased. 'Granny's cat has got kittens, you know, and I shall see them, if she hasn't given them all away yet. Oh, Mummy, I do so wish we could have one.'

But Mother didn't like cats, and she shook her head. 'No, dear. Don't keep asking me that. Now hurry up and go.'

Daisy soon got to Granny's. She kissed the old lady's soft, wrinkled face and then asked about the kittens.

'They've all gone but one, the prettiest of the lot,' said Granny. 'It's the little white one. Now where is the little kitten? Call it.'

'Kitty, kitty, kitty!' called Daisy, but the kitten didn't come. Daisy looked everywhere for it. She looked under the bed, under the couch and out in the garden. Only Tabby, the big mother cat, was there, sitting washing herself on the wall.

'Where's your white kitten?' asked Daisy, but Tabby took no notice at all. Daisy thought her kittens were much nicer than she was. Tabby never played at all.

'I can't find the kitten, Granny,' said Daisy sadly. 'I'm sorry I can't, because I'm sure next time I come it will be gone.'

'I'm sorry you can't find it,' said Granny. 'It's always hiding away somewhere. Now you had better go back, darling, because it is getting late.'

'What about the homemade sweets for Mummy's sale, Granny?' asked Daisy. 'She said I was to bring them back.'

'Oh, yes,' said Granny. 'I've got everything ready in this basket. I've put the boxes of sweets at the very bottom, and above them I have put some knitted gloves and hot-water bottle covers I have made for Mummy's sale too. The basket is quite light, so you can easily carry it.'

Daisy picked it up. She kissed Granny goodbye and went down the path. Granny had given her one of her homemade bits of toffee, and Daisy sucked at it as she went.

The basket was quite heavy. It dragged at Daisy's arm, and she took it in the other hand. 'Dear me,' she said, 'it feels very heavy, although Granny said it was light. I shall be tired when I get home!'

She found her mother when she got home. She put the basket on the table, and Mother kissed her. 'You're a good, helpful little girl,' she said, 'and I shall give you something out of Granny's basket for a reward. Another toffee, perhaps – or a pair of knitted gloves – or a piece of Granny's chocolate fudge. You can choose what you would like.'

'I'll unpack the basket for you,' said Daisy, and she lifted off two hot-water bottle covers beautifully knitted by Granny. And then Daisy got such a surprise!

The little white kitten lay curled up in the basket, settled cosily on the knitted gloves! It had crept in there when it felt tired and had fallen fast asleep. It opened big wondering eyes and stood up to stretch itself.

'Oh, Mummy! I brought the kitten home and I didn't know it!' cried Daisy. 'Oh, isn't it sweet?'

The kitten leapt lightly on to the table. It rubbed its soft little head against Mother's hand.

'Mummy, it loves you!' cried Daisy. 'Oh, Mummy, you said I could choose anything out of Granny's basket for a reward – could I, could I have the little white kitten?'

'Miaow,' said the kitten, and rubbed its head against Mother's hand again. She simply couldn't help loving it back.

'Yes, you can have it,' she said. 'It's too sweet for words. I don't like cats, but I've lost my heart to this kitten. I'll ring Granny and tell her we'll keep it if she'll let us!'

'Oh, thank you!' said Daisy. 'No wonder the basket felt heavy. You're mine, kitty. How will you like that?'

'Miaow-*ee-ow-ee-ow*,' said the kitten. And Daisy knew what that meant! 'I shall love being your kitty; you're such a nice little girl!'

Catch Him Quick

# Catch Him Quick

'WOULD YOU like to see my pet white mice, Ian?' asked Alice when Ian came to tea one afternoon.

'Ooh, yes,' said Ian. 'I'm not allowed to keep pet mice – but I wish I was. I do like them.'

'I'll get mine. They're called Bubble and Squeak,' said Alice. 'I'll bring them up to my playroom. You wait here.'

She had soon brought the two white mice in their little cage. They were so tame that they ran all over Alice and Ian, and twitched their little pink noses as they sniffed about here, there and everywhere.

'Oh, I do wish I had two lovely little mice like

these,' said Ian. 'I really do.'

After a while Mother called out that their tea was ready. 'We'd better put the mice back into their cage and go,' said Alice. 'We'll play with them again afterwards.'

The two mice were quickly put back into their cage. Alice swung the little door shut and latched it. Then they went downstairs to have their tea.

But Alice hadn't latched the door properly. It swung open – and the mice were easily able to get out! Squeak didn't want to get out. She was always afraid of cats when the playroom was empty. But Bubble was much bolder. He ran out at once.

The toys had been very interested in watching the two mice while the children were playing with them. Now when Bubble came running out the sailor doll sat up in a hurry.

'Catch him quick! He's escaping! The children will be very upset if they find him gone.'

'Catch me if you can!' said Bubble and scampered

about the playroom floor. The sailor doll chased him. The teddy bear tried to head him off. The curly-haired doll tried to trap the naughty mouse in a corner.

But the mouse was much too clever to be caught. He ran here, he ran there – he laughed at the toys, and not one of them could manage to catch him.

'There he goes. Catch him quick!' shouted the sailor doll again as the mouse rushed out from under the couch.

Off they all went after the mouse. Just as they thought they had finally got him he slipped away again.

'Can't catch me! Can't catch me!' he called.

The sailor doll stopped, out of breath. He thought hard for a minute. Then a big grin spread over his handsome face.

He whispered to the bear. 'I've got an idea. I'm going to hide behind the curtain where no one will see me. And I'm going to make a noise like a cat!'

'Ooooh, Sailor Doll! That is a good idea!' said the bear. 'That will give the naughty little mouse such a fright. He will go rushing back to his cage at once!'

The sailor doll slipped quietly behind the curtain. Then he began to mew. 'Miaow-*ee-ow-ee-ow*! Miaow! Miaow!'

The mouse stopped short at once and looked around anxiously for the cat. But he couldn't see it anywhere.

'Miaow-*ee-ow*!' mewed the sailor doll, trying his hardest not to laugh.

The mouse gave a squeal and looked at his cage. Dare he run right across the floor to it? Would the cat catch him as he went across? Well, he must try.

He scampered across the floor – and the sailor doll mewed again. The scared mouse turned aside and ran into the doll's house! The little front door was open, so he got in easily.

'He's in the doll's house! Quick, shut the door!' yelled the bear. 'You dolls in the doll's house, shut all the windows quick! Don't let that naughty mouse out!'

The curly-haired doll slammed the door of the house shut. The tiny dolls inside the house shut all the windows. Now the mouse was well and truly caught. He couldn't get out.

He went to a window and peeped out. 'Where is that horrible cat?' he said, twitching his nose up and down very fast.

Nobody said a word. The mouse flew into a rage. 'I don't believe there ever was a cat! I didn't see one! I do believe it must have been one of you mewing, not the cat!'

The sailor doll giggled. He really couldn't help it. Then Bubble knew for certain that a trick had been played on him and he scampered up and down the little stairs in the doll's house, trying to get out. But he couldn't.

What a furious rage he was in! He was so angry that he scared the tiny dolls and they had to get into the bedroom wardrobe to hide.

Then Alice and Ian came back into the playroom. They went to the mouse's cage and Alice gave a small scream.

'Oh, no! The door of the cage is open! I do hope the mice haven't escaped!'

Squeak was there, of course – but Bubble wasn't. So the two children began to hunt about all over the playroom.

Alice was nearly in tears. 'He was so sweet. I did love him. Oh, Bubble, where have you gone?'

Bubble heard Alice's voice and he pressed his little pink nose against a window in the doll's house, trying to see where Alice was – and quite suddenly she saw him!

'Oh, look, isn't that Bubble in my doll's house? Yes, it is, it is – looking out of the window. Oh, Bubble, you look sweet in there. But you must come back to your nice, safe, cosy cage with Squeak.'

The children looked at one another. 'You know,' said Alice, 'there's something strange about this, Ian. I know the door and windows of my doll's house were open, because I opened them myself this morning. Well then, who shut them when Bubble got in?

Whoever was it that caught him there?'

They looked around at the toys sitting so still and quiet in the playroom. Alice looked hard at the sailor doll.

'He's got a wider smile than usual on his little face!' she said. 'Sailor Doll, I'm sure you caught the mouse. Thank you very much. I shall let you go home with Ian to play with his toys as a reward.'

So he did, and when the sailor doll came back he had quite a few stories to tell the other toys. It was a good reward for him, wasn't it?

# Pinkity's Party Frock

# Pinkity's Party Frock

PINKITY WAS a pixie who loved to go to parties. She went to the rabbits' parties and to the mouse picnics. She loved going to the fairies' parties, and, dear me, what a treat it was to go to a party at the palace.

Pinkity lived in Jenny's garden – but Jenny didn't know! Pinkity had a tiny house under the old lilac bush. All the mice knew it well and so did the two rabbits who lived at the end of the garden. One of the hens knew it too, for she had gone under the bush to lay an egg. But Jenny didn't know, though she had played round the bush a dozen times a day!

Jenny played with her doll Rosebud. She loved her

very much, for Rosebud was a pretty, cuddlesome doll, whose eyes shut to go to sleep and who could say 'Mama' in a very baby-like voice. Rosebud had two lots of dresses – a pink silk one with a white sash, and a blue cotton one for mornings.

Pinkity often used to watch Jenny playing with Rosebud. One day, as Pinkity was peeping through the leaves at Jenny the postman came with a letter for the pixie. The postman was a little mouse. Pinkity took the letter in excitement.

'I hope it's a party invitation!' she cried. And it was! It was from the fairy Goldywings, and the party was to be the next day, Monday; a picnic party on Breezy Hill.

'Oh, what fun!' cried Pinkity. 'I shall make myself a dress and hat of pink rose petals. I *shall* look fine!'

That night she went to collect the pink rose petals from Jenny's garden. She came across old Shellyback, Jenny's tortoise, lying asleep in the grass.

Pinkity laughed. 'I shall use you for a stool to sit

on!' she said. So she sat down on the tortoise's back, and began to make her pink frock and hat. First she made the hat and fitted it on her head. Really, it looked very pretty all made of silky petals. Then she began to make the frock.

She worked till dawn, and then she had to go and fetch some more pink thread from her little house. So she dropped the little frock lightly on to the ground by the tortoise and ran off.

When she came back whatever do you think had happened? Why, the old tortoise had awakened, and put his head out of his shell. He had seen the rose-petal frock – and had begun to eat it up!

You see, rose petals were a great treat to him. He loved a feast of them and didn't often get them. So when he saw the rose-petal frock he began to gobble it up in delight!

Well, poor Pinkity sat down and cried and cried when she saw what was happening! 'You horrid unkind thing!' she sobbed. 'I've spent all night long making my new frock – and you eat it in about two minutes!'

'Sorry!' said Shellyback. 'I didn't know it was a frock. I thought it was just rose petals and I'm very fond of them.'

'It's Monday morning now and there won't be time to make myself a frock again,' sobbed Pinkity. 'I shan't be able to go to the picnic this afternoon!'

'I'm very sorry,' said Shellyback again. He did wish he could do something!

Pinkity slipped back to her house under the bush, still crying. Shellyback pulled at the grass and waited for Jenny to come out to play.

When she came out she looked very important. It was Monday – and she was going to have a washing day just like Mother! She had washed Rosebud's pink-silk frock and her white petticoat and vest, and had washed her pram cover and pillowcase too. Now Mother had put her up a little clothesline in the garden to hang the things on to dry!

The tortoise watched Jenny pegging up all the clothes. He wished he could tell her about Pinkity, but he had only a hiss for a voice and Jenny wouldn't understand.

Jenny went indoors then to get her hat and coat for a walk. Shellyback watched the clothes flying on the line and went on eating.

The wind blew hard. It blew the little clothes on the little line and it blew Mother's big clothes on the big line. It blew so hard that it blew the pink-silk frock off the line altogether, and it flew off and wrapped itself round the tortoise's head!

He *was* surprised! He put his head into his shell at once. Then he poked it out again to see what it was that had dropped on him.

It was Rosebud's best pink-silk frock – and the tortoise stared at it in excitement. Just the thing for Pinkity to wear at the picnic! If only it would fit her!

Shellyback picked the frock up in his mouth and crawled under the lilac bush with it. Pinkity was there, still crying. How she stared when she saw the tortoise bringing the pink-silk frock!

'Oh! Oh! Where did you get it from?' she cried. 'What a beautiful dress – and I believe it will just fit me – and will match my new rose-petal bonnet beautifully!' She slipped the frock over her head and tied the white sash round. How sweet she looked!

'Oh, thank you!' she said to Shellyback, kissing his little blunt nose. 'I'll wear it to the picnic!'

She ironed it out, and then put it on for the picnic with her pretty pink bonnet. Off she went as happy as could be – and how every one admired her in her pretty silk frock!

Poor Jenny *was* upset when she came in from her walk and found the pink-silk frock had been blown off the line. She hunted and hunted for it – but, of course, she couldn't find it!

Then it was *her* turn to weep!

The tortoise heard her crying and soon knew why. How uncomfortable he felt! First he had eaten

Pinkity's rose-petal frock and made her cry – and now he had taken away Jenny's doll's frock and made her weep. He went to the lilac bush and waited for Pinkity to come home. When she came he told her how upset Jenny was.

'Oh, dear!' said Pinkity. 'What a shame! Well, I'll soon wash and iron this frock, Shellyback, and then I'll give it back to Jenny for Rosebud. And I'll give her my rose-petal bonnet too. It should fit the doll nicely.'

So that evening Pinkity washed and ironed the pink frock, and then packed it up in a little box, with the pink bonnet too. She flew up to the nursery window, slipped in at the top and left the box on the table.

When Jenny found it and opened it the next morning she could hardly believe her eyes! 'Oh, look!' she said. 'Here's my doll's frock back – and a lovely rose-petal bonnet too! It will just fit Rosebud.'

So it did, and she wears it every time she goes out.

Jenny would so love to know who made it. Shellyback has told her heaps of times, but she doesn't understand his hisses. I wish I could tell her, don't you?

# A Tale of Sooty
# and Snowy

# A Tale of Sooty and Snowy

DOWN AT the toyshop there was a big black cat with eyes as green as cucumbers. She belonged to Mrs Kindly, who owned the toyshop, and her name was Comfy. This may seem an odd name for a cat, but it was exactly right for Mrs Kindly's cat. Comfy looked just like her name – cosy and comfortable and warm. All the children loved her.

Comfy used to sit on the counter near the teddy bears and fluffy rabbits, and the boys and girls stroked her when they came into the shop.

Two children liked her especially. They were a brother and sister called Robert and Ruth. They always stroked Comfy to make her purr. She had a very loud purr indeed.

'It's as loud as Mummy's sewing machine!' said Robert.

Mrs Kindly always liked to see Robert and Ruth in her shop. They were so nice to one another. They seemed to share everything. They even shared stroking the big black cat.

'Your turn to stroke her now,' Ruth would say to Robert.

If ever they had any money to spend, they shared it out between them too. 'Our uncle gave me a sixpenny piece,' said Robert. 'And he gave Ruth a box of sweets, Mrs Kindly. So Ruth shared the sweets with me, and now I'm going to share the sixpence with her. That's threepence each. Have you anything for threepence?'

'It's a pity more brothers and sisters aren't like you two,' Mrs Kindly often said. 'Now take John and Jane – the unkind things they say to one another! And Peter and Pam – why, I had to send them out of my shop the other day, they quarrelled so!'

Now one day Comfy the cat wasn't on the toy counter with the rabbits and the bears when Robert and Ruth came in.

'Oh! Where's Comfy?' asked Ruth.

'I'll show you,' said Mrs Kindly, and she took Robert and Ruth to the little room at the back of her shop. By the fire was a cosy basket, and in it was the big black cat, Comfy. She purred loudly when she saw the two children.

'Look what she's got in her basket!' said Mrs Kindly, and the children looked.

Ruth gave a squeal. 'Oh! Kittens! How many? Aren't they simply lovely!'

'She's got two,' said Mrs Kindly, 'and the odd thing is that one is black just like Comfy herself, and the other is white. They will make a pretty pair later on.'

The kittens were very tiny. They hadn't even got their eyes open yet. They snuggled up to their big soft mother, and she licked them lovingly.

After that, of course, Robert and Ruth came to see the kittens every single day. They watched them grow, and they were glad when they opened their blue eyes. Then the kittens began to crawl about the basket and make funny little squeaky mewing noises. The children loved them!

They told their mother about the kittens – and Comfy the cat talked about the two children in mew language to her kittens.

'They're nice children,' she told the kittens. 'Brother and sister, just like you are, Snowy and Sooty. And you must see that you are as kind and good to one another as Robert and Ruth are.'

She didn't really need to tell the two kittens that, because they loved one another from the first day that they opened their eyes and saw each other! They played and cuddled together, and shared the ball of wool that Mrs Kindly found for them to play with. When they were old enough to drink milk they shared the same saucer, and they ran everywhere together.

'We should really call them Robert and Ruth!' Mrs Kindly said to the two children one day. 'They are just like you two. Dear little Snowy and Sooty, I shall be sorry when I have to sell them. So will their mother cat; she loves them so.'

Comfy was upset when she heard Mrs Kindly say that. Good gracious! So her kittens would be sold – and, not only that, the two would be parted from one another. One would go to one home and the other to another home. They might never see one another again!

Snowy and Sooty cuddled together and mewed into each other's furry ears. 'Let's always keep together. Let's not go to different homes. Let's stay together like Robert and Ruth.'

But, oh, dear, Mrs Kindly soon put a notice in her window. It said:

TWO BEAUTIFUL KITTENS FOR SALE:
ONE WHITE, ONE BLACK.

'You'll soon be parted now,' said their mother to them sadly. 'Nobody ever wants two cats – so make the most of one another because you never know when someone will come in and buy one of you.'

Robert and Ruth saw the notice in the shop window. They did hope nobody would buy the kittens yet – they really were so sweet now. Robert loved Sooty and Ruth loved Snowy. Each child took up a kitten and petted it.

'I shall just hate to hear that someone has bought Snowy and taken her away,' said Ruth, her voice trembling. 'I do so love her.'

'And I shall hate to know that someone has bought Sooty,' said Robert. 'He's so amusing and so quick and so cheeky! I love him too.'

Now when Robert got home that day he went to his moneybox to see how much money he had. The kittens were two shillings and sixpence each. If he had five shillings he would buy them both!

But he only had a half crown, made up of a shilling,

two sixpences, a threepenny-bit and three pennies. And by the time he could save up another two shillings and sixpence both kittens would have been sold.

He thought longingly of Sooty – black as soot, green-eyed now like his mother, playful and loving. He had enough to buy him.

But Ruth loved Snowy. If he were going to buy a kitten, he would have to buy Snowy, because Ruth loved her – she would be disappointed if he bought Sooty. It was a puzzle to know what to do!

He went out to sit in the shed and think about it. When he was gone Ruth came running into the playroom and she took down her moneybox. She had had exactly the same thought as Robert. Had she enough money to buy both kittens? That would be lovely!

She counted out her money. Two shillings, a sixpence, three threepenny-bits and a penny. How much was that? Surely it would be nearly five shillings! But it wasn't, of course. It was only three shillings and fourpence – what a shame!

Ruth put the money back. Then she too went to think about things in the woodshed. Robert had just gone. Ruth sat down and thought much the same thoughts as Robert.

*If I buy Snowy for myself – and I do so love Snowy – Robert will wish and wish it was Sooty, because he loves Sooty. But I haven't enough money for both!*

She thought again, sitting on a pile of sacks, frowning. Then she jumped up.

*Well, I love Snowy, but I love Robert more! I'll go and buy him Sooty for a very great surprise! How pleased he'll be!*

Her mother called her as she ran indoors to get her money. 'Ruth! Just come and help me untangle my wool for a minute.'

'Where's Robert?' asked Ruth, holding out her hands for the wool.

'He ran out in a hurry,' said her mother. 'He said he was going down to the village for something.'

Well, I don't know whether you can guess where

Robert had gone. Yes, to the toyshop! Was he going to buy Sooty because he loved him so?

No, he wasn't. He was going to buy Snowy for Ruth! What a pair! Robert wanted Sooty, but he was going to buy Snowy instead – and Ruth wanted Snowy, but she meant to buy Sooty because Robert liked him so.

Robert was in the toyshop with his money in his hand. He spoke eagerly to Mrs Kindly. 'Mrs Kindly! Has anyone bought Snowy yet? Because I want to buy her.'

'Nobody's bought Snowy,' said Mrs Kindly. 'But, dear me, Robert, I thought it was Sooty you liked.'

'Yes, I do, but I'm buying Snowy for Ruth,' said Robert. 'Please don't say a word, Mrs Kindly – it's a surprise!'

'Well, well,' said Mrs Kindly, 'you're a generous fellow, Robert. We'll go and get Snowy now. Dear me, the two kittens will be sad to part. They're just as much to one another as you and Ruth are!'

Snowy was picked up and put into a basket with a lid. Mrs Kindly lent it to Robert to take Snowy home safely. Snowy mewed sadly.

'Goodbye, mother cat, goodbye, Sooty! Oh, Sooty, I do hope we see each other again! Goodbye!'

'There, she's saying goodbye to her mother,' said Mrs Kindly. 'And to her brother – how those kittens will miss each other!'

Robert carried the kitten home carefully, sorry for Sooty left behind, but glad to think of how delighted Ruth would be. He went in at the back door just as Ruth ran out of the front one, her money clutched in her hand. She had finished untangling the wool and was going to buy Sooty for Robert!

She ran to the toyshop and burst in at the door. 'Mrs Kindly,' she said, 'has anyone bought Sooty, please? I do so want to buy him.'

'But I thought you liked Snowy,' said Mrs Kindly.

'Oh, I do – but Robert loves Sooty, you see. I'm buying him for Robert,' said Ruth. 'I've only enough money for one kitten.'

Mrs Kindly led the way into the room at the back of the shop. Sooty was there, alone with his mother, mewing sadly.

'Where's Snowy?' asked Ruth. 'Oh, has someone bought darling little Snowy? Oh, I did so want to say goodbye to her before anyone took her! Poor little Sooty – he's missing Snowy already. Oh, dear, if *only* I'd had enough money to buy both kittens. Has Snowy gone to somebody kind, Mrs Kindly?'

'Dear me, yes – to one of the kindest persons I know,' said Mrs Kindly, smiling and longing to tell Ruth who had taken Snowy. But Robert had asked her to keep his secret, so she didn't tell Ruth any more. The little girl borrowed a basket from Mrs Kindly and Sooty was put into it, mewing loudly.

'He wants Snowy,' said Ruth, almost in tears. 'Don't cry, Sooty. I want Snowy too, but there wasn't enough money.'

She took Sooty home carefully. She carried him

into the playroom where she could hear Robert whistling. She held the basket behind her back, her eyes shining. And there was Robert, holding something behind his back too! It was the basket with Snowy in. He had been anxiously waiting for Ruth to come back.

'I've got a present for you – guess what it is!' said Ruth.

'And I've got one for you!' said Robert. 'Guess!'

Well, they didn't have to guess, because at that very moment Sooty and Snowy smelt one another's furry smell and mewed in excitement, calling to each other.

'Miaow, MIAOW!'

And when the children put the two baskets on the table out jumped Sooty and Snowy who ran to each other at once, rolling over and over in delight!

'Why, you've bought Sooty!' cried Robert joyfully.

'And you've bought Snowy!' said Ruth. 'Oh, Robert, and I did so wonder who had got Snowy – and it was you! You'd bought her for me. Thank you, thank you, thank you!'

Mother came in to hear what all the excitement was about – and how surprised she was to see a snowy-white kitten and a sooty-black one playing together.

'What a lovely pair!' she said. 'Whose are they?'

'Ours!' said Robert and Ruth together. 'Oh, Mummy – we're so happy!'

So were the two kittens. They couldn't believe that they weren't to be parted after all. Robert and Ruth still have them, though they've grown into lovely big cats now. They often sit on the windowsill inside the sitting room, side by side, and passersby see them and stare. 'What a pretty pair!' they say. 'There ought to be a story about them!'

So there ought – and that's why I have written one for you!

Rover's
Hide-and-Seek

# Rover's Hide-and-Seek

ROVER WAS a very clever dog indeed. He could balance biscuits on his nose, toss them up into the air and catch them neatly in his mouth. He could shut the door and always waited for the click that told him it really was shut – and he could fetch Father's paper for him, and pay for it! He took the money in his mouth, and brought the paper back in his mouth too.

Another thing he could do was play hide-and-seek. You should have seen him! It was marvellous to watch him. He would stand behind a bush and wait patiently there while Mary or Peter hid themselves. He didn't shut his eyes – but he never looked round, because he wasn't a cheat.

Then when the two children had hidden themselves they would call, 'Cuckoo! Cuckoo!' Rover would at once bound away from the tree and go to look for the children! He always found them no matter where they hid. Father said he smelt where they went. He was really very clever.

He did love playing with Mary and Peter. Often he would go to their playroom and scrape at the door.

'Woof!' he said. 'Woof!'

'There's Rover!' Mary would say. 'He's come to ask us to play with him! Come on, Peter. Let's play hide-and-seek!'

Now one day Mary and Peter went out with their father. He wanted to take them to the zoo, and they were most excited.

'Can we take Rover too?' asked Peter. 'He always comes with us, wherever we go, Daddy.'

'No, we can't take him to the zoo,' said Father. 'Dogs are not allowed at the zoo. You wouldn't like him to fight a lion or a tiger, would you, Peter? Or try to make friends with a polar bear?'

'Well, Daddy, let's creep off without Rover knowing,' said Mary. 'He will be so upset if he sees us going off without him, really he will!'

So, while Rover was having a nice, crunchy breakfast of biscuits in the kitchen, the three slipped away out of the front door. Rover didn't know they had gone at all. He went on with his breakfast quite contentedly, planning to have a good game of hide-and-seek with Mary and Peter afterwards.

When he had finished he went upstairs to the playroom. He scraped at the door. He found that it was open a little so he went in. To his surprise there were no children in there. Wherever could they be? Downstairs, perhaps, trying to get a piece of cake from Mother!

So down went Rover and found Mother. But she was doing the ironing and she was rather cross.

'Shoo! Shoo!' she cried. 'Get out, Rover, I'm busy!'

Rover went into the garden, puzzled. Wherever in the world could those children be?

Then, as he stood by the old apple tree he heard a call, 'Cuckoo! Cuckoo!'

*Of course*, thought Rover, his tail beginning to wag hard. *They're playing hide-and-seek! Why didn't I think of that? They were both hiding somewhere. I'll go and find them. I heard them calling 'cuckoo'! It sounded as if it came from the end of the garden.*

Down he trotted and smelt about by the wall there. But he could neither smell nor see the children. It was most puzzling. He held up his head and listened to see if he could hear them talking.

'Cuckoo! Cuckoo!' he heard.

*Tails and whiskers, that sounds as if they are up by the garden shed!* thought Rover in surprise. *How could they have got from the bottom to the top of the garden without my seeing or hearing them?*

He ran to the garden shed and looked inside and out. No children! No smell or sound of them either! It was really most strange. Rover couldn't understand it.

'Cuckoo! Cuckoo! Cuckoo!'

Rover listened in astonishment. Well, this time it sounded as if the children were calling to him from the front garden! He trotted there and hunted thoroughly. No, they were not there either!

Poor Rover! What a day of hide-and-seek he had to be sure. You see he didn't know or guess that the cuckoo had come back that day, and was calling merrily all round about! He had quite forgotten about that bird. He really and truly thought it was the children calling him as they always did when they played a game of hide-and-seek with him.

By the time that Mary and Peter came back, Rover was quite tired out. He had hunted everywhere, in all the places where the cuckoo call seemed to be coming from. Mother could not think what was the matter with Rover. Whatever was he looking for, and why did he listen with his head on one side so often?

But when Peter and Mary came home from the

zoo and heard what Rover had been doing – and heard the cuckoo calling too – they guessed at once what had happened.

'Poor, darling old Rover!' said Mary, hugging him. 'So you played hide-and-seek with the cuckoo all day long, did you, old fellow? What a shame! Never mind – we'll have a proper game tomorrow, and you really will find us this time!'

Rover wagged his tail. He was still very much puzzled – but nothing mattered now that he had his dear little master and mistress back again.

They played hide-and-seek the next day – but, you know, the cuckoo did spoil it for them. He would call 'cuckoo' *before* they were ready! I think he must love to play hide-and-seek too, don't you?

# Snubby's Tail

# Snubby's Tail

SNUBBY WAS a fat little guinea pig. He was perfectly tame and lived in a nice hutch in Leslie's garden. He had plenty to eat and a lovely soft bed to lie on, so he was very happy.

At least he was very happy till he got out of his cage one night and met Frisky the squirrel, who was scampering about in the moonlight, having a fine game.

'Hallo there!' said Frisky in surprise. 'What sort of animal are you? I've never seen a creature like you before.'

'Oh,' said Snubby, 'well, I don't really know what I am. I am called Snubby.'

'Snubby!' said Frisky. 'Well, I've never heard of snubbies before! So you are a snubby? Let's have a look at you.'

He bounded all around Snubby and then roared with laughter. 'You've come out without your tail!' he said. 'Where is it?'

'My tail!' said Snubby, astonished. 'Oh, dear! Haven't I got one on?'

'No,' said Frisky. 'What have you done with it? Have you lost it?'

'I must have,' said Snubby sadly, looking at Frisky's beautiful bushy tail.

'We'll ask people if they have seen it,' said Frisky, and he took hold of Snubby's front paw and went off with him. 'Look! There's Mrs Quack! Let's ask her!'

They went up to a large white duck who was busy diving for food in a nearby pond. She stared at Snubby in surprise when she saw him, for she had never seen such a creature before.

'This is a snubby,' said Frisky. 'He has lost his tail. Look!'

Mrs Quack looked. 'Dear, dear!' she said. 'So he has. What a pity!' She wagged her own feathery tail to make sure she had it, and Snubby did wish he had one like hers.

'I haven't seen the snubby's tail,' she said. 'But Willie the dog is somewhere about, hunting rats. He may have seen it.'

So Snubby, Frisky and Mrs Quack went off together to look for Willie the dog.

He was hunting rats and had his head down a hole. He had a fine long tail that wagged when the others spoke to him. Snubby did wish he had a tail like that.

'Hallo, hallo!' said Willie, pulling his head out of the hole and looking at the others. 'What's all this? Whatever is this interesting creature?'

'It's a snubby,' said Mrs Quack and Frisky together. 'Isn't he curious! He hasn't a tail – look! He must have lost it. We wondered if you had seen it.'

'No, I haven't,' said Willie. 'But there's an old rat tail he can have if he likes.'

'No, thank you!' said Snubby at once. 'I'm not going to have a tail like that! I want one like Frisky's – or like Mrs Quack's, or yours, Willie!'

'Oh, well!' said Willie. 'If you're going to be so particular, I'm afraid I can't help you! I haven't seen your lost tail!'

'Don't be cross, Willie,' said Frisky. 'You are a clever dog – just think hard for a minute and see if you can think of some way to get back the snubby's tail!'

So Willie thought hard. Then he woofed and said, 'Of course! There's the wishing well! If we can get old Mother Turnabout to come with us to the well, she can get Snubby's tail for us!'

So off they all went to Mother Turnabout's. She was knitting by the fire, and was most astonished to see Snubby, Frisky, Mrs Quack and Willie walking in at the door.

'Bless us all!' she cried. 'What's this? Now what

have you come for at this time of night?'

'Please, Mother Turnabout, will you come with us to the wishing well and wish back the little snubby's lost tail for us?' begged Frisky. 'He lost it coming along tonight, and he is so miserable without it.'

'I've never heard of a snubby before,' said Mother Turnabout, peering at Snubby through her spectacles. 'Funny little chap, he looks! Well, I'll come, but mind you, creatures, I shall want an egg from you, Mrs Quack; a score of nuts from you, Frisky; and you'll please guard my house for me for a week, Willie. As for you, little snubby thing, I don't know if you lay eggs or what you do – but when you've got your tail back you can repay me in some way!'

They all went out of the door and made their way to the old wishing well in Mother Turnabout's garden. She took a shiny green stone and dropped it down the well. Then she spoke softly. 'Well, wishing well, are you listening? Bring back the tail of the little snubby!'

She let down a bucket into the water, and then

slowly pulled it up again. She put her hand into the bucket to get out the tail she expected to find there.

'How very strange!' she said at last. 'There is no tail here! This is the first time that the wishing well has ever failed to grant a wish! I must let the bucket down again!'

Down it went again – and up it came again – but there was no tail there! Mother Turnabout grunted, and walked back to her cottage, sad and puzzled.

All the creatures followed her, quite frightened. The old dame sat down in a chair and frowned.

'I can't make it out!' she said. 'Why didn't it grant my wish? Surely, oh, surely, the magic hasn't gone out of my wishing well!'

She stood up and went to the door. She called loudly, 'Cinders, Cinders, Cinders!'

A big black cat with green eyes came bounding up. He was astonished to see Mother Turnabout's visitors, and he spat rudely at the dog.

'Cinders!' said the old dame. 'I wished for a tail of

this little snubby to come back, for he lost it this evening – and it didn't come back!'

'Then he didn't lose it,' said the cat.

'But he must have!' cried Mrs Quack, Willie and Frisky. 'He hasn't got it on!'

'Let me see,' said the cat. So Snubby came forward and then turned himself slowly round backwards. Sure enough, he had no tail.

But Cinders looked at him closely – and then he began to laugh, showing all his sharp white teeth.

'What's the matter?' cried everyone.

'Why, that's a guinea pig and they don't have tails!' said the cat. 'He didn't lose his tail – he never had one! Ho, ho, ho! What a joke!'

'You said he was a snubby!' cried Mother Turnabout angrily to Frisky.

'He said he was!' said Frisky.

'I didn't! I said my name was Snubby, and so it is!' cried Snubby, quite frightened. All the animals looked so fierce that he made up his mind to run – and out of the door he went as fast as his four little legs could carry him.

'After him!' cried Willie – and out they all went, leaving Mother Turnabout in her chair, feeling very glad indeed to think that the magic hadn't gone out of her well after all!

Snubby hid under a bush and Mrs Quack, Willie and Frisky ran by. Then out he crept and ran back to his hutch as fast as he could. How glad he was to be there once more! He shut the door with his own snubby nose and was pleased to hear the click that told him it was latched. He was safe!

*I don't want a silly tail!* he thought. *If you have a tail, you have to keep a wag in it, and that would be such a nuisance. I'm lucky to have no tail!*

And he went to sleep and dreamt that Mother Turnabout had stolen Frisky's tail, and Willie's tail and Mrs Quack's as well, and had put them all onto her best Sunday hat. How he laughed when he woke up! Funny little Snubby!

# The Lucky Jackdaw

# The Lucky Jackdaw

ONCE UPON a time there was a little girl called Fiona, who lived with her aunt and uncle. One day she found a baby jackdaw on the ground. He had fallen from a nest in the church tower and couldn't fly back.

'You poor little thing!' said Fiona. 'I'll take you home and look after you till you're well enough to fly away.'

So she took him home and found a cardboard box that she stuffed with hay. She put the little black creature into it and then went to find some bread and milk.

'Good gracious!' said her aunt. 'Whatever will you

bring into the house next? You brought a stray cat last month, which stole the joint out of the larder. Last week you found a stray dog with a bad leg, and it chased our chickens as soon as it got better. Now you've got a wretched little jackdaw who will steal everything shiny and bright he can lay his beak on, as soon as he can fly!'

'Oh, please, Auntie, let me look after him,' begged Fiona, who was so kind-hearted that she really couldn't leave any small or hurt creature by itself. 'I'll keep him in the shed outside if only you'll let me look after him. I'm sure he'll fly away as soon as he's big enough.'

'Very well,' grumbled her aunt. 'I suppose you can keep it if you like. But if that bird steals any thimbles of mine, I'll punish you, so there!'

So Fiona kept the jackdaw in the shed outside. She had to feed it many times a day, for it was a hungry little thing. She put bread soaked with milk on the end of a pointed stick, and the small creature took it greedily.

Jack grew very quickly, and soon had a pair of strong black wings. But he didn't fly away! He was so fond of Fiona that wherever she went he went too, and even if she went for a walk, the jackdaw flew along with her, circling round her head and calling, 'Chack! Chack! Chack! Chack!'

Then he began to be naughty. He went into the house one day and saw Fiona's aunt sewing. She put her bright thimble down for a moment, and Jack caught it up in his beak. In a second he was out of the window, and had hidden the thimble in a hole right up in the thatch.

'Oh, you wicked bird!' cried Fiona's aunt. 'Bring me that thimble back at once! Fiona! Fiona! Where are you? That jackdaw of yours has taken my thimble! I told you that was what would happen!'

Fiona called Jack and made him bring back the silver thimble. Then she scolded him hard, and he sat on the fence and hung his head.

But it didn't make him mend his ways. Whenever he saw anything bright and gleaming he picked it up in his beak and flew off with it. Fiona's aunt was angry, and she said she wouldn't have Jack in her shed if he didn't stop his wicked ways.

Fiona was very miserable. She was fond of Jack and couldn't bear to think that he might have to leave. Her aunt scolded her, not because she was a nasty lady, but just because she was very worried about a lot of things.

'Your uncle hasn't been able to work for a month because of his bad leg,' she said. 'And the hens are not laying and the cows are not giving enough milk. Where is the money going to come from to pay the rent? I really don't know. The shoemaker wants his bill paid too. You'll have to help me a little more, Fiona, to make up for that horrible bird of yours always worrying me. I'm sure he took the money I put on the dresser yesterday.'

Poor Fiona! She worked hard from morning to

night to help her aunt. She fed the hens and milked the cows, she looked after her uncle and did everything she possibly could. She begged her aunt not to get rid of her jackdaw, but her aunt wouldn't promise.

'If only the bird would pay you back for your kindness to it!' she said. 'If it was a hen, it could lay eggs! But it just does nothing but steal things.'

Now the jackdaw knew that the aunt hated him, and he was very unhappy. He flew off by himself one day and came to a buttercup field. He fluttered down to the river that flowed through it, and as he walked down to the water to have a drink something very bright caught his eye.

It was a ring. It lay in the water near the bank, and seemed to wink at him as the stream went rushing over it. Jack thought it was very pretty indeed. He put his head into the water and pulled out the ring.

It shone even more brightly. It had three great big shiny stones in it, and Jack pecked at them. But they were held tightly in the ring, and he could not get them out. So he decided to take the ring back home with him and show it to Fiona.

Off he went. Fiona was sitting peeling potatoes with her aunt, and they were talking together.

'Mr Brown told me this morning that Lady Penelope went out in a boat on the river yesterday and lost her beautiful diamond ring,' said Fiona's aunt. 'I expect that it will never be seen again. They say it is worth a lot of money.'

'Is it worth as much as a hundred pounds?' asked Fiona.

'Oh, the ring will be worth much, much more than that!' said her aunt. 'Why, there's a reward of a hundred pounds offered to anyone who manages to find it.'

When Jack heard this he gave such a squawk that Fiona's aunt jumped and dropped her potato knife on the floor.

'There's that horrible bird again!' she said. 'I'll have someone take him away tomorrow, I really will!'

Jack squawked again and hopped up to her. He dropped the ring right into her lap and then stood with his head cocked on one side to see what she would do with it.

The woman picked up the diamond ring and looked at it in the greatest astonishment. For a moment she could hardly speak. Then she found her tongue. 'Fiona!' she said. 'Fiona! I do believe this is the ring that Lady Penelope lost! Your jackdaw must have found it in the river!'

'Oh, Auntie!' cried Fiona in delight. 'Then we shall get the hundred pounds! And you can pay the rent and the shoemaker and the doctor, and you'll have plenty of money left over!'

'Put on your coat and come with me to the house where Lady Penelope lives,' said her aunt in great excitement. So Fiona got her coat and then she and her aunt set out for the big house that belonged to Lady Penelope. Jack went along too, flying round their heads and shouting, 'Chack! Chack!' as loudly as he could. And for once Fiona's aunt didn't scold him.

At last they arrived at the house. The butler took them into a big room, and Lady Penelope came in to see them. As soon as she saw the ring, she cried out with joy and took it from Fiona's aunt.

'Wherever did you find it?' she cried. 'What part of the river was it in?'

'Our jackdaw found it,' said Fiona.

'Chack! Chack!' called the jackdaw, flying to the window. Lady Penelope thought he really was the cleverest bird she had ever seen.

'I found him when he was a baby,' said Fiona. 'I looked after him till he was big, but he wouldn't fly away. He stayed with me all the time. Sometimes he is very naughty, but now he really has been very good we shall have to make a fuss of him! You won't want to get rid of him now, will you, Auntie?'

'No,' said her aunt. 'He really has paid you back for your kindness to him, Fiona!'

'And I must pay you your reward!' said Lady

Penelope. 'I will send the money this evening when I have been able to get it from the bank.'

Off went Fiona and her aunt again, very, very happy, for all their troubles were gone. The jackdaw knew they were glad and he shouted loudly all the way home.

The money came that day. Fiona's aunt paid all her bills, bought some more hens and a pretty new dress for herself. Fiona had two new dresses and a pair of shiny blue shoes.

They wanted to give Jack a present too, but all they could think of was a little bit of nice fresh meat, which he ate greedily.

Fiona's aunt never said another word against him. In fact, she became very fond of him, and after that she always let Fiona look after any stray animal or bird that she found, so the little girl was very happy.

As for Jack he lives with them still – but if you go to see Fiona, be careful not to leave your money about! He is still very naughty at times!

# The Tale of Kimmy-Cat

# The Tale of Kimmy-Cat

THERE WAS once a cat called Kimmy-Cat who loved going fishing. He fished in his master's goldfish bowl and caught six little goldfish and ate them. He was scolded for that, but *he* didn't care! He just waited till more fish were put in the bowl and then he fished for those and ate them too!

Then he found his way to the neighbour's pond, and waited patiently by the water until a very big and beautiful fish came by. Out went Kimmy-Cat's paw, and the poor fish was caught and eaten.

Kimmy got into trouble for that, and he was punished. The other cats laughed at him.

'Fancy going fishing!' they said. 'You *are* a silly, Kimmy-Cat! Why, you have nice fresh codfish cooked for you every day, and yet you go catching those poor goldfish. We think you are a naughty cat.'

'Goldfish taste so nice,' said Kimmy-Cat. 'You just come with me and taste them.'

But none of the other cats would do such a naughty thing. So Kimmy-Cat had to go alone. He didn't dare to go to the pond next door, so he roamed away by himself to look for another one.

Soon he came to a wood, and right in the very middle of it he found a perfectly round pond with pink water lilies growing on the surface.

But better than water lilies to Kimmy-Cat was a big fish, very golden and with bright diamond-like eyes. It swam slowly about the little pond, and shone like gold.

'Ho!' said Kimmy-Cat to himself. 'That's the fish for me!'

He crouched down and waited until the fish came

near the bank. Then in a flash he shot out his paw and caught it. It landed on the bank, and wriggled to get away from him. But Kimmy-Cat got its tail into his mouth, and was just going to start eating the fish, when a voice shouted at him, 'Leave that fish alone! You wicked cat, drop that fish at once!'

Out of a little cottage came a small man in red with a pointed cap on his head. Kimmy-Cat saw that he was very tiny, so he took no notice of him. But the little man ran right up to him and took the fish away. He slipped it into the water and it swam off, none the worse for its adventure.

'You bad cat!' said the little man. 'Haven't you been taught not to go fishing? It's as bad as stealing to go fishing in other people's ponds. That goldfish is my pet, and I've had it for twenty years.'

'I've a good mind to sit here and catch it again,' said Kimmy-Cat.

Suddenly the little man looked closely at Kimmy-Cat's tail – and then he began to laugh and dance about in glee!

'Ho, ho, ho!' he shouted. 'You've eaten a tiny bit of my fish's tail, and won't you be sorry for it! My fish is magic, and you'll be sorry you ever touched it! Ho, ho!'

Kimmy-Cat looked at his tail. Then he looked again – and, oh, dear me, whatever was this? His own tail was vanishing, and he was growing a fishtail instead!

Kimmy-Cat looked at it in horror. Even as he watched it grew bigger and bigger. At last his own tail was completely gone – and in its place was a fine fishtail, golden bright and double-pointed.

'Oh, my!' said Kimmy-Cat in dismay. 'What a dreadful thing! Here, little man, change it back at once!'

'I can't!' said the little man, still capering about in delight. 'No one can take it away for you, because it's magic. You'll have to go on wearing it – and every fish you eat will make it grow bigger still!'

Kimmy-Cat gave a loud 'miaow', and ran away in fright. This was the worst thing that had ever happened to him! He ran all the way home and curled himself up in his basket before any of the other cats could see him.

But they smelt his fishtail and came crowding round him, thinking he had got a fish in his basket. The dogs came too, and so did the cook.

'Have you got a fish there?' she said sharply. 'You know that the master forbade you to go fishing any more, you naughty cat. Get up and let me see if you have a fish!'

But Kimmy-Cat wouldn't move. He didn't want anyone to see his fishtail. The cook suddenly became cross, tipped him out of his basket – and then stared in the greatest surprise at his tail!

'Good gracious, what's this?' she cried. 'Why, what have you done to your tail, Kimmy? It's a fishtail!'

All the cats and dogs sniffed at it, and then they began to laugh.

'No, Kimmy's turning into a fish because he catches so many!' they said. 'Look at his tail! He's half a fish!'

Kimmy-Cat went very red indeed. He curled up in his basket again, and pretended to take no notice. But soon more cats came up and more still, all attracted by the fishy smell in Kimmy-Cat's basket. In despair Kimmy-Cat jumped out and ran away.

But that was no use either – for wherever he went the cats nearby smelt fish and ran after him. How Kimmy-Cat wished he had never gone fishing!

At last he went back to the little man and begged for his help.

'I couldn't help you even if I wanted to, which I don't,' said the little man. 'The best thing you can do is to hide away until your own tail has grown again. It will take about a month, I should think.'

'But where can I hide?' asked poor Kimmy-Cat.

'Well, you can hide in my little house here, if you like,' said the man. 'But in return for that you must do all the work in my house for me. That will be very good for you, for I can see that you have thought of nothing and nobody but yourself up till now. You are too disobedient and unkind.'

Kimmy-Cat said nothing. He at once went indoors and found an apron to put on. Then he took a broom and began to work hard.

His own tail began to grow again. It gradually pushed the fishtail away, and at last, by the time the month was nearly up, there was nothing left of the fishtail except for a tiny spike at the end of his own furry tail.

Kimmy-Cat was so glad. He had learnt a lot. He was a different cat when he said goodbye to the little man and went home again.

'Here comes Kimmy!' cried all the other animals. 'Where have you been, Kimmy-Cat? Where's your fishtail?'

'It's gone,' said Kimmy-Cat. 'Please don't talk of it to me, my friends. I am a good cat now, and all I want is to be kind and friendly.'

'We will be nice to you!' said the cats and dogs at once. 'If you will be nice to us, we will never say a word about the fishtail, not one! Come and have some cream! And there's some nice boiled codfish that Cook has got ready for us.'

'I'd like the cream – but not the fish!' said Kimmy-Cat with a shudder. And I'm not surprised, are you?

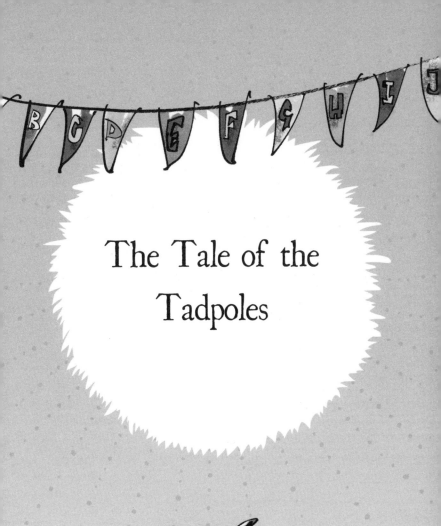

# The Tale of the
# Tadpoles

# The Tale of the Tadpoles

THERE WAS once a small boy called Timmy. He went fishing one day in a little pond where some frogs had laid their eggs. They had laid them in jelly, but now, in the warm sunshine, the jelly had melted, and the eggs had hatched out into tiny black tadpoles.

How they wriggled and raced around the pond! They were strange things, all tail and head. Timmy wondered what they were. He put some in a jar and took them home, with some pondweed for them to cling to if they wanted to.

'Look, Mummy!' he said. 'What are these? Haven't I got a lot of the little black wrigglers?'

'Yes, you have. Far too many,' said his mother. 'Now, Timmy, you like frogs, don't you? Well, these tiny wrigglers will all change into frogs, if you take care of them properly. It will be like magic.'

'Gracious! I'd like to watch them turning into frogs,' said Timmy, who couldn't imagine how they did it. 'But have I really got too many, Mummy? I'd like a lot of frogs, you know.'

'Well, if you do what most children do and keep dozens in a small jar, they will all die, for there will not be enough air in the water for them all to breathe,' said his mother. 'Take all but five or six of them back to the pond, Timmy, and just keep those few.'

So Timmy kept five in his jam jar and watched them carefully. His mother showed him how to tie a tiny bit of food on a thread and hang it in the jar for them to nibble at. Then he pulled it out again so that it would not go bad and make the water smelly and cloudy. He left the pondweed in because the tadpoles loved that.

One day he put them out in the jar in the sun. The hot sun warmed the water, and soon the tadpoles rose to the top, turned over and looked as if they were dying. Timmy rushed to his mother at once.

'Oh, Timmy! They're slowly cooking in the sun, poor things!' said his mother, whipping them away to a cool corner and putting a little cold water into the jar. 'Poor creatures! I hope they won't die. Hundreds of poor little tadpoles are cooked every year because children put them into the hot sun!'

'I didn't think,' said Timmy sadly. 'I do hope they'll be all right, Mummy. I do like them so very much.'

They didn't die. They got better when they felt cool. So Timmy was able to watch the magic that turned the tadpoles, all heads and tails, into tiny frogs with four legs and a little squat body! Their back legs grew, and then their front legs. Their tails became short. Timmy watched them each day, so he knew. He gave them a cork to climb on when they became tiny frogs, for now they liked to breathe the air.

Then he put them into his garden so that they could find new homes for themselves.

'Eat the grubs and flies for me,' he said. 'I've been a friend to you – now you can be a friend to me!'

Would you like to see frog magic too? Well, do as Timmy did then and keep a few tadpoles in a jar.

Master Prickly

# Master Prickly

JOAN WENT out into the garden one morning, carrying her tennis racket and some balls. She meant to have a fine game all by herself on the tennis court.

She lifted the net that ran all round the court – and then she stopped in surprise.

Something heavy was caught in the edge of the net. Whatever could it be?

Joan knelt down to see – and then she gave a cry. 'Mother! Come here! Some little creature has rolled itself up at the bottom of the net, and can't get out.'

Mother came running to see. 'Oh, it's a hedgehog!' she said. 'Poor little thing! It must have come hurrying out last night to look for the special toadstools it likes, or some slugs or beetles to eat – and has run into our net. Its prickles became caught in it, and the more it struggled, the tighter it was tangled!'

'Oh, dear – can we get it out? Is it hurt?' asked Joan.

'Not hurt, but scared!' said Mother. 'Well, we can't possibly untangle the net, Joan – it's wound so tightly round the little thing's body. Go and get my scissors and we'll cut the net.'

So they cut the strands, and bit by bit freed the frightened hedgehog. At first he didn't move at all – then he suddenly uncurled himself and looked at Mother and Joan out of bright little eyes.

'He's very, *very* prickly, isn't he?' said Joan. 'Why does he grow so many sharp prickles, Mother?'

'Because no enemy will eat a prickly animal!' said Mother. 'How would *you* like a mouthful of prickles, Joan?'

'I wouldn't!' said Joan. 'Mother, he's got such a dear little snout – and such bright black eyes. I like him. I'd like him for a pet.'

'Well, he wouldn't be a very *cuddly* pet,' said Mother. 'And also, I don't expect he would want to stay in one place. He'd soon wander away again.'

'What does he do in the wintertime?' asked Joan, feeling how sharp the hedgehog's prickles were.

'He makes himself a warm little bed of dead leaves and moss in a hole in a bank,' said Mother. 'And he sleeps and sleeps and sleeps!'

'Do you suppose he's hungry?' asked Joan. 'Oh, look, he's *quite* uncurled himself now and he's running about. Can't we give him something to eat?'

'Hedgehogs love bread and milk,' said Mother. 'You go and get him some, and I'll watch that he doesn't run away before you come back.'

As soon as Joan stood up to go, the hedgehog curled himself into a ball in fright. It was marvellous to see him! It didn't take Joan long to fetch the bread and milk, and she set it down gently beside the rolled-up prickly ball.

'Now come a little way away,' said Mother, and they quietly moved off a few yards. In half a minute the hedgehog uncurled himself again and stood on his four short legs. He sniffed the air – what could he smell?

He ran over to the bread and milk, and to Joan's delight he began drinking the milk greedily, and pulling out bits of the soaked bread to eat.

'Now listen, Joan, I believe if we put out a saucer of fresh bread and milk each day, we would perhaps get Master Prickly to stay with us,' said Mother. 'He seems really very tame! Shall we try?'

Well, it was just as Mother said – Master Prickly, as they called him, *was* very tame, and he soon became used to Mother and Joan. He looked for his saucer of bread and milk each day, and every time Joan put it out, she placed it just a *bit* nearer to the house, so that it would be easy to see the hedgehog from the windows.

'He's a real pet now, isn't he, Mother?' said Joan

one day. 'I'd like him to be mine – and pay for his milk each day myself.'

'Well, you can if you like,' said Mother. 'Look, here comes Granny. Granny, come and see our pet hedgehog!'

Granny came over at once. 'What a dear little fellow!' she said. 'Would you lend him to me, Joan, just for a night or two?'

'Whatever for, Granny?' asked Joan in surprise.

'Well, my cellar is full of horrid black beetles!' said Granny. 'They come out each night, and Cook won't go down there to fetch anything then – nor will I! We can't bear beetles.'

'Will Master Prickly get rid of them for you then?' asked Joan.

'Good gracious, yes!' said Granny. 'He'll gobble them all up in no time! If you lend him to me, I'll pay you sixpence a time – that will pay for his bread and milk, won't it?'

'Oh! Then Master Prickly will be paying for it

himself!' said Joan, pleased. 'He'll be earning his own living. Prickly, what do you think of that? Aren't you a clever hedgehog?'

He certainly was. In two nights he had cleared Granny's cellar of all the black beetles there, and she was delighted. She gave Joan a shilling.

'Look, Prickly!' said Joan. 'It's for you – to buy your dinner each day! Well done!'

Joan will be sorry when he goes to sleep for the winter, won't she?

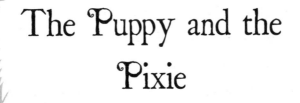

# The Puppy and the Pixie

# The Puppy and the Pixie

BOBS WAS a puppy dog, a black spaniel with long floppy ears. He lived with his master and mistress in a house on the hillside, and he loved to go rabbiting among the holes up and down the hill.

He didn't catch a rabbit, but he liked to put his nose down a hole, and then scratch and scrape with his front paws until he had made quite a pile of earth outside. He felt most important then.

One day he went off by himself to sniff down a very large rabbit hole he had found under a gorse bush. He snuffled and scraped, as excited as could be – and then he suddenly felt a sharp pain in his right fore paw.

'Woof!' said Bobs, holding up his paw. 'What is it?'

He licked his paw, but still it hurt him. He thought he would run home to his mistress and ask her to make his paw better – but when he tried to run down the hillside he found that he could not put his paw to the ground because it hurt him so much. He tried to run on three legs, but even then he kept forgetting and putting his hurt paw to the ground.

So he sat down on the grass and howled loudly. He was only a puppy and he was frightened. He had never been hurt before and he couldn't understand it. Why did his paw hurt so badly? He had licked it and licked it, but it still hurt whenever he trod on it.

'*Wow-wow-wow-wow!*' he whined. '*Wow-wow-wow-wow-wow!*'

Then he heard a small voice speaking to him from a piece of bracken nearby. 'What's the matter?' You woke me up with your howling, puppy dog. Why do you make such a noise?'

Bobs looked up in surprise. He saw a small pixie

swinging in a hammock made of a bracken frond. She was dressed in silvery cobwebs and had a harebell for a hat.

'Hallo!' said Bobs in surprise. 'Who are you?'

'Just a pixie,' said the little creature. 'I live on the hillside, and brush and comb all the baby rabbits for their mothers. They keep me busy early each morning, I can tell you. But what's the matter with you? Why did you make such a dreadful noise?'

'I'm sorry I woke you up,' said the puppy. 'But something is the matter with my paw. It hurts when I walk on it.'

'Let me see,' said the pixie, and she jumped lightly out of her bracken hammock. She ran up to the puppy and lifted up his paw.

'Why, you've got a gorse thorn in it,' she said. 'You poor thing! No wonder it hurt you to walk. Let me get it out for you.'

'Don't hurt me,' said the puppy.

'I shan't hurt you a bit,' said the pixie. 'There! It's

out! Look what a nasty long thorn it was.'

The puppy looked – and, dear me, what a long prickle the pixie had taken out of his foot! It was like a big needle. The little creature took a fine white handkerchief from her pocket and neatly wrapped up his paw.

'There!' she said. 'Now you'll be all right.'

'You *are* kind!' said Bobs gratefully. 'I hope some day I will be able to do you a good turn too.'

'I don't expect you will,' said the pixie, climbing back into her hammock. 'You'll forget all about me in a few days.'

But Bobs didn't forget. He often thought of the kind pixie and her gentle hands. He kept the little handkerchief she had wrapped round his paw and put it right at the back of his kennel to remind him of the pixie who had made his paw better for him. Every time he smelt it he thought of her and hoped one day he would be able to do her a kind turn too.

The months went by. Summer was over and the

autumn came. All the leaves fell off the trees, and the bracken on the hillside turned bright brown. Bobs wondered if the pixie was still there, but when he went to look he couldn't see her anywhere.

Then winter came – and a very hard winter it was too. The snow fell every day and soon the hillside was white from tip to toe. Bobs had a kennel outside in the yard, and his mistress filled it full of warm hay and straw, and turned it away from the wind so that he would be warm. He was as warm as toast on the coldest night, and loved his cosy kennel.

One night he heard a sound in the yard, and he pricked up his ears. It was someone sighing and sobbing.

'Oh, my, oh, my, the cold is dreadful! There is no warm place to go. Oh, I shall die of the cold, I'm sure.'

Bobs knew that voice! He rushed out of his kennel and almost knocked over a small pixie standing shivering in the middle of the yard.

'Be careful, you great clumsy thing!' she cried

crossly. 'You nearly sent me flying into the snow, and goodness knows I'm cold enough without falling head over heels in a snowdrift.

'Pixie, pixie, it's Bobs, the puppy whose paw you made better in the summertime,' said the dog eagerly. 'Have you come to see me?'

'No,' said the pixie, shivering. 'I didn't know you lived here. I've had to leave the hillside because it was so very cold. But I've nowhere to go and I'm sure I shall freeze to death.'

'Come and live with me!' said Bobs. 'I'd love to have you.'

'But you live indoors in a basket, don't you?' said the pixie.

'No, I've got a nice little house of my own called a kennel,' said Bobs. 'It's just here in the yard, very warm and cosy. Come along. We can cuddle up together and be as warm as toast.'

He took the shivering pixie to his warm kennel and she crept gratefully into the soft hay there. She cuddled up to him and very soon was warm from head to foot.

'This is lovely,' she said. 'I haven't been so warm for weeks. Oh, if only I could stay here!'

'Well, you can,' said Bobs. 'My mistress wouldn't mind a bit if she knew. She would be pleased. You know, pixie, I always said I would like to do you a good turn to repay you for taking the thorn out of my foot – and I'm so happy to be able to. You will be company for me, and as soon as the warm days come again, you can go back to the woods if you like.'

So there they live in the warm kennel together, Bobs and the pixie, as cosy as a pie. Would you like to see the pixie? Well, if you know a dog called Bobs, go and peep into his kennel when he is not there. You *might* see the pixie then, right at the back, sleeping soundly in a little bed of straw.

Surprise for Mother
and Susan

# Surprise for Mother
# and Susan

ON THE bookcase was a round glass bowl full of water. In it, swimming about in some strands of green water weed, was a fine goldfish.

He belonged to Susan. She loved Goldie. She fed him, saw that he had some nice weed in his bowl all the time, and once she gave him two water snails for company. But they ate his weed so she took them out.

Goldie wasn't at all lonely. He liked talking to the toys when the nursery was empty. They all liked Goldie too. He swam round and round his bowl, and sometimes he poked his nose right out of the water.

'I do wish you'd come right out and play with us!'

said the sailor doll. 'Why don't you?'

'Well, I have to live in water,' said Goldie. 'I'd like to come and play with you, really I would – but, after all, I've no legs or arms, so I wouldn't be much fun.'

'You could slither along the floor,' said the sailor doll. 'Do come.'

But Goldie wouldn't. He didn't mind poking his nose out of the water now and again, but he didn't think he would like to get right out.

'Susan's got a toy goldfish that swims in her bath at night,' the panda told Goldie one day. 'Susan puts him in when the bath is full and takes him out again when it's empty. He lies there in the soap rack all day and he doesn't seem to mind. If he can live out of the water, why can't you?'

'I don't know. I just don't want to get out of my bowl,' said Goldie rather crossly.

'He's just silly,' said the sailor doll, getting cross himself. 'He won't try!'

Now when the sailor doll made up his mind that

he wanted something he went on and on until he got what he wanted! And he suddenly made up his mind he wanted Goldie to get out of his bowl. But how could he make him?

He thought of an idea at last. *I'll get the toys to have some sports*, he thought. *Yes, running and jumping for prizes. I'll offer the prizes. I've got a sweet hidden at the back of the cupboard. And there's a bit of red ribbon I found in the wastepaper basket. That will do for another prize.*

The toys were quite excited when they heard about the sports. The panda helped the sailor doll to arrange them. The toys had to run round the nursery to race one another. They had to see how high they could jump over a rope. And they had to choose partners for a three-legged race too.

'I'll give a prize for that,' said the panda. 'I've got a brooch out of a cracker. I'll offer that as a prize for the three-legged race.'

'Goldie ought to go in for the sports too,' said the sailor doll.

'Don't be silly,' said the panda. 'He can't run. And how could he possibly go in for the three-legged race when he hasn't got even one leg?'

'But he could jump,' said the sailor doll. 'He could jump high out of the water. He could jump right out of his bowl! We could easily put him back. If we thought he had jumped the best, we could give him the prize. He would look nice with the red ribbon round his neck.'

Goldie couldn't help feeling rather excited when he heard all this. He pressed his nose against the glass of his bowl, and tried to see all that was going on.

The sailor doll climbed up on the bookcase. 'Do you want to go in for the jumping prize?' he asked Goldie. 'I bet you could win it! I once saw you jump a little way out of your water, and it was a very good jump. Don't you want a red ribbon?'

'Well, I'll go in for the jumping,' said Goldie. 'Yes, I will! You tell me when it's my turn.'

The sports were to be held that night. The

toys were excited. They started off with the running race and the toy rabbit easily won that. He simply galloped round and came to the winning-post long before the others. He was very pleased with the sweet for a prize. It was a bit old and dirty, but he didn't mind.

'Now for the jumping,' said the sailor doll. 'And let me tell you, toys, that the goldfish is going in for this too! My word, I guess he'll jump high!'

All the toys took their turn at jumping. The kangaroo out of the Noah's ark jumped the highest of all.

Goldie popped his head out of the water. 'I can jump higher than the kangaroo – I can, I can!' he called in his bubbling voice. 'Watch me!'

He jumped high out of the water – very high indeed! But, alas, when he fell back he struck the edge of the bowl and bounced over on to the bookcase instead of back into the water.

He slithered from the bookcase, and fell over the

edge. Thud! He crashed to the floor, and lay there wriggling and gasping.

'I can't breathe!' he gasped. 'I can't breathe out of water. Put me back quickly, or I shall die.'

The toys were horrified. The panda rushed to him, but he couldn't get hold of Goldie, he was so slippery. And even if he could hold him, how could he possibly get him back up to the top of the bookcase?

Goldie wriggled hard on the carpet. 'Water, water!' he gasped. 'Water, get me water!'

'Sailor Doll! Tell us what to do. *You* made poor Goldie jump!' cried the toys.

The sailor doll was almost crying. He had got his way. He had made Goldie jump out of his bowl. Now he wanted nothing better than to get the poor goldfish back into his water. How could he have been so foolish and unkind as to try to make him jump out?

'Go on, Sailor Doll, do something!' shouted the toys. 'It's your fault; it's your fault!'

'I can't climb up the bookcase with Goldie; I can't,' sobbed the sailor doll. 'He's heavy and slippery.'

'I know what you can do! I know!' squeaked the rabbit. 'Look, there is a bowl of flowers on the table. You can climb up the chair, surely, and then on the table. Quick, pick Goldie up in your arms and climb up. Quick, quick!'

The poor goldfish was hardly wriggling at all now. He lay on the carpet, gasping, his mouth opening and shutting feebly. The toys couldn't bear to see him like that.

The sailor doll picked him up. He was wet and slippery and heavy. The sailor managed to climb up on to the chair seat with him, with the toys helping him. Then up on to the table he went, panting and sobbing. He ran to the flower bowl. It was a deep green bowl and Mother had put some green sprays in it, for there were few flowers out so early in the year.

The sailor doll flung the goldfish into the bowl of greenery. He slid down into the water. At once he felt better. He wriggled feebly at first, taking in great gulps of water and then felt stronger.

The toys all climbed up on the table to watch. They saw Goldie flap his tail and fins rather feebly. Then they saw him wriggle himself – and then they saw him try to swim, opening and shutting his mouth as he always did.

'Goldie, dear Goldie, are you all right now?' asked Panda. 'Do you feel better?'

'Yes, much better,' said Goldie, coming to the top of the water and poking his nose out between the stems. 'But I do think it was mean of the sailor doll to make me go in for the jumping. He might have known I would fall out and crash down to the floor.'

'I wanted you to fall out; I wanted you to come and play with us,' said the sailor doll, wiping his tears away. 'I thought if only I could make you jump out, you'd be quite all right, and could come and join our games. I didn't know you would die out of water.'

'Now I'm in a pretty fix,' said Goldie. 'All mixed up with these stems. And the water doesn't taste very nice either. Panda, did I jump high? I haven't even got a prize.'

'You shall have the red ribbon,' said the sailor doll at once. 'Come up to the top and I'll tie it round your neck. You really do deserve it, Goldie. Nobody jumped so far as you – right out of the bowl and down to the floor! Gracious, no one else would dare to jump off the bookcase.'

Goldie couldn't help feeling pleased to have the prize ribbon round his neck. He felt very grand and important. He swam in and out of the stems, looking very fine.

The toys went back to the toy cupboard. The night went and the morning came. And in the morning Susan ran into the nursery. She looked at the goldfish's bowl as she always did – and stared in astonishment.

'It's empty!' she cried. 'Where's Goldie? Oh, surely he hasn't jumped out and died.'

But he was nowhere on the floor – nowhere to be found at all! Susan ran to tell her mother. Together they hunted about for Goldie. But they couldn't find him.

'Well, lay the breakfast, dear,' said Mother at last. 'Goldie's gone. Goodness knows where to!'

Susan laid the breakfast, feeling very sad. She and her mother sat down – and then her mother gave a cry of surprise.

'Susan! Look, Goldie's in the flower bowl! How *did* he get there? Did you put him there?'

'Oh, Mummy, *no*! Of course not!' said Susan in astonishment. 'I've been very miserable about him. Mummy, he *is* in the flower bowl – he's swimming about among the stems!'

Mother and Susan watched Goldie in amazement – and then Susan saw the ribbon round his neck. It was very limp and wet, of course – but, still, it was a ribbon.

'Oh, Sue – you *must* have put the ribbon round his

neck and popped him into the flower bowl to give me a surprise!' said Mother. And she simply wouldn't believe that Susan hadn't done it.

But Susan knew she hadn't. She looked round at her toys, and she saw that the sailor doll was wet all down the front of him. He winked at her.

*It's something to do with the sailor doll*, thought Susan. *It is, it is! But what? If only he could talk to me. Now I'll never know what happened!*

You can tell her if you ever meet her. But I'm not sure she'll believe you. Wasn't it a surprise for Susan and her mother?

# Mr Twiddle and
# His Wife's Hat

# Mr Twiddle and His Wife's Hat

ONE DAY Mrs Twiddle wanted to take her hat back to the hat shop because she didn't like the red roses on it.

'I would much rather have violets on my new hat,' she said to Mr Twiddle. 'Don't you think violets would be nicer than roses, Twiddle?'

'Well, dear, hollyhocks and sunflowers are very beautiful too,' said Mr Twiddle, looking out into his garden proudly, where his hollyhocks were flowering very tall and straight, and his giant sunflowers were growing as high as the house, though they were not yet out.

'Twiddle! Do you think I would put hollyhocks and sunflowers on a hat?' cried Mrs Twiddle. 'Do, for goodness' sake, think what you are saying!'

'I *was* thinking,' said Mr Twiddle, offended. 'And I think that sunflowers and hollyhocks are—'

'All right, all right!' said Mrs Twiddle quickly, because she didn't want to hear it all again. She picked up her new hat with red roses.

'You don't think it would be nice to have feathers on my hat instead of flowers, do you?' she asked.

'No, I don't,' said Mr Twiddle, who was very fond of birds and hated to see their feathers in people's hats. 'Why don't you have mouse tails or something like that? I wouldn't mind seeing mouse tails on your hat at all.'

'Twiddle, don't be horrid,' said Mrs Twiddle. 'You know how afraid of mice I am. I should run miles if I had their tails on my head.'

Mr Twiddle thought it would be fun to see Mrs Twiddle run miles. He began to think how he could get some mouse tails for her. But Mrs Twiddle didn't give him any time to think.

'I shall go back to the shop now,' she said. 'You come with me, Twiddle, there's a dear, and you shall help me to choose new flowers for my hat. You can carry the hatbox for me too. That will be a great help.'

'Very well,' said Mr Twiddle. He watched Mrs Twiddle put her hat carefully into a box full of white tissue paper.

'You tie the box up for me, Twiddle, while I go and get ready,' said Mrs Twiddle. Off she ran, and Mr Twiddle looked around for some string. There was none in the string box, of course. There never was. Mr Twiddle thought he had some in the woodshed outside, so out he went.

Now when the kitchen was empty Mrs Twiddle's big black cat walked in. He simply loved playing with paper of any sort, so when he saw the white tissue paper sticking out of the hatbox he ran over to it at once. He pulled at it and the lid fell off. That made him jump. He crouched back, and then sprang at the box. He landed right inside it, on top of the hat.

'Miaow-*ee-ow*!' said the cat, pleased. He began to play with one of the red roses. He burrowed right underneath the white paper. He had a simply lovely time!

Mr Twiddle was a long while finding the string. The cat played with the roses till he was tired. Then he settled down inside the hat, with all the tissue paper on top of him. He tucked his nose into himself and went to sleep. He loved sleeping on paper.

Presently Mrs Twiddle bustled into the room, all ready to go out. She called Mr Twiddle. 'Twiddle, Twiddle! What in the world are you doing? I'm just going to get my coat.'

Mr Twiddle came running in with a long piece of string. 'I've been hunting for string,' he said. 'Really, this is a dreadful house for string. Never a bit to be found!'

'Well, hurry and tie up the hatbox,' Mrs Twiddle

said impatiently. 'You always take such a time over doing everything!'

Mr Twiddle put the lid on the box quickly. He tied it up firmly. He picked up the box and set off after Mrs Twiddle, who was already walking down the garden path.

The box felt very heavy. *Surprisingly heavy*, Mr Twiddle thought. He simply couldn't understand it. How brave women were to wear such heavy hats on their heads! He began to puff and pant.

'Twiddle! What are you puffing like that for?' Mrs Twiddle cried in surprise. 'It's not such a hot day as all that, surely!'

'Your hat is so heavy,' said poor Mr Twiddle, who didn't know he was carrying a very large cat as well as the hat.

'Twiddle! How can you say that my little straw hat is heavy?' said Mrs Twiddle. 'What a fuss you do make! I'm ashamed of you.'

Mr Twiddle went redder than he already was. He

hated Mrs Twiddle to be ashamed of him. He took the box in both arms and panted along. But really it was frightfully heavy.

'I shall have to have a rest, dear,' said Mr Twiddle when they came to the seat by the bus stop. 'This box is so very heavy really.'

'I hate stopping here,' said Mrs Twiddle. 'The bus seat is just outside the fish shop, and I don't like the smell.'

But Mr Twiddle meant to have a rest, so he sat down, putting the box on his knee to leave room for other people on the seat. Mrs Twiddle sat down too. She turned up her nose at the smell of the fish in the fish shop.

The cat woke up when he smelt the fish. He was very fond of fish. He thought it would be nice to taste some, so he began to wriggle around the box to find a way to get out.

Mr Twiddle was rather alarmed. The box seemed to be coming alive! It moved on his knee. It shook and wriggled. Mr Twiddle held it tightly, for he really thought it was going to jump off his knee.

'What's the matter now, Twiddle?' said Mrs Twiddle, noticing that Mr Twiddle looked frightened.

'Well, my dear, your hat is not only very heavy but it seems to be walking around the box,' said poor Mr Twiddle.

'Walking around the box!' cried Mrs Twiddle. 'Whatever will you say next? You know perfectly well that a hat can't walk around a box.'

'It seems to be jumping up and down in the box now,' said Mr Twiddle, beginning to tremble. The cat was doing his very best to get out. He mewed quietly a few times.

'The hat is talking,' said Mr Twiddle. 'I'm glad it's not my hat. I wouldn't wear a heavy, talking, walking, jumping hat like this for anything!'

The cat suddenly went quite mad and began to leap round and round the box, scratching at the paper as he went. Mr Twiddle couldn't bear it any longer. He dropped the box into the road!

Mrs Twiddle jumped up with a scream. 'Oh, my new hat, my new hat!' she cried, and she ran to get it. She picked up the box and took it back to the seat. It did feel very heavy. It did feel as if the hat was leaping about. How very extraordinary! Mrs Twiddle undid the string with trembling fingers and took off the lid.

Out leapt the big black cat with a howl, scratched Mrs Twiddle on the hand and flew off down the road with his tail straight up in the air!

'Was that a cat or my hat?' wept poor Mrs Twiddle, putting a hanky round her hand.

'It was your cat,' said Mr Twiddle, glaring after the running animal. 'That cat! He's always getting into mischief. Now perhaps you will say you're sorry to me for making me carry your cat such a very long way!'

'Well, perhaps you'll say you're sorry to me for putting a cat into my hatbox, and letting it sit on my new hat!' sobbed Mrs Twiddle, taking a very squashed hat out of the box. 'He's chewed the roses!'

'I shan't say I'm sorry, but I'll buy you some new violets for the hat,' said kind Mr Twiddle, who was upset to see his wife so unhappy. 'Come along.'

'Well, I shan't say I'm sorry then, but I'll buy you a kipper for your tea,' said Mrs Twiddle, wiping her eyes.

So Mrs Twiddle had her violets and Mr Twiddle got his kipper – but, as I dare say you will guess, the big black cat got nothing at all except a good scolding when he came in to sniff at the kipper!

# The Lost Slippers

# The Lost Slippers

DADDY WAS very pleased because Mummy had given him a beautiful new pair of slippers for his birthday. They were bedroom slippers, very soft to wear, and lined inside with brown wool.

'Aha!' said Daddy, putting them on. 'Now my feet will be warm!'

Peter and Betty wished they had slippers like Daddy too.

'Mummy, our slippers are wearing out,' Betty said. 'Couldn't we have some small ones like Daddy's big ones? We would so love to be like Daddy!'

'Very well,' said Mummy. 'I will buy you some next

week when we go by the shoe shop.'

So very soon not only Daddy had nice warm bedroom slippers, but the two children had as well. They put them on and danced around the nursery in them.

'Look!' Betty cried to Cinders, the black cat. 'See my new slippers!'

'Look!' Peter called to Spot, the little terrier puppy. 'Don't you wish you had slippers like mine, Spot?'

Every night Daddy put his slippers on when he got home, and every night the two children put theirs on when they went upstairs to bed. Betty's were blue with brown wool inside, Peter's were yellow and Daddy's were brown.

And then a strange thing happened. The slippers began to disappear! First, one of Betty's went.

Mummy was cross about it.

'Haven't I told you, Betty, to put your slippers away carefully when you get into bed?' said Mummy.

'But I *did*, Mummy!' cried Betty.

'Well, you couldn't have,' said Mummy. 'Or they would both be under your chair this morning.'

That night one of Daddy's slippers disappeared. It was really most mysterious. Nobody could understand it! Betty had put both Daddy's slippers to get warm by the fire – and when Daddy came in and sat down in his chair to take off his shoes there was only one slipper for him to put on!

'Hie, Betty!' he called. 'Where's my other slipper, darling?'

'Isn't it by the fire, Daddy?' said Betty in astonishment. 'I put it there.'

'Have you been having a joke and hidden it, Peter?' asked Daddy. Peter was fond of playing tricks, and Daddy thought it might be Peter who had run off with the slipper for fun. But Peter shook his head.

'No, Daddy, I haven't touched your slippers, really I haven't.'

'Well, it must be about the room somewhere, that lost slipper!' said Daddy. 'Hunt about and find it.

Perhaps it is under my chair.'

The two children hunted about everywhere, but they could *not* find Daddy's slipper. So he had to put on his old ones, and he was quite cross about it.

The next slipper to disappear was one of Peter's! Yes, it really did. Peter knew quite well he had put them carefully under his chair when he got into bed – but the next night one was gone! Only one slipper stood under his chair.

'I say! This is getting a bit *too* mysterious,' said Peter. 'Is it magic, do you think, Betty?'

'I don't know,' said Betty, puzzled. 'It's so strange, Peter, because anyone who wanted the slippers to wear would take *both* – not one! All our slippers are different sizes – one is no use to anyone!'

Mummy was annoyed about the slippers. 'They *must* be somewhere!' she said. 'Betty and Peter, you must just hunt about everywhere today till you find them. It must be carelessness. There is no other explanation!'

'Come on, Cinders; come on, Spot, and help us to hunt for the slippers!' said Peter. So the cat and the dog and the two children hunted everywhere for the lost slippers.

They looked under all the beds. They lifted all the chairs. They hunted in every cupboard. They even looked in the larder, though Cook said if they found any slippers there, she would be *most* surprised. They didn't, of course.

Then they went to look behind the cushions. No, no slippers were there either. It was most puzzling.

Cinders and Spot trotted all over the place with the children, sniffing here and there. At last the children came to the shelf on which stood the three remaining slippers – one of Daddy's, one of Betty's and one of Peter's. They did look funny, all odd, by themselves.

Spot ran up to one of the slippers and took it into his mouth. He threw it up into the air, caught it and then began to shake it like a rat. Then he ran off to his big, cosy basket with it.

'Hie, Spot, don't *you* steal any of our slippers!' cried Peter, and he ran after the puppy.

But Spot quickly tucked the slipper under his warm rug and lay down on it, all his legs in the air!

'Betty! Perhaps *Spot* has taken our slippers!' cried Peter. He ran to the basket, and tipped the puppy out. Then he lifted up the big, warm rug – and what do you suppose he saw? Yes, you are quite right! All the lost slippers were there, as well as the one that Spot had just taken! There they were, neatly tucked under the rug, all a bit chewed.

'Mummy! Mummy! We've found the lost slippers!' cried Peter. 'Come and look!'

So Mummy came and when she saw where they were how they laughed – and how they scolded the naughty puppy!

'We must keep them where he can't get them!' said Mummy. So now all the new slippers are kept safely in a cupboard, and Spot isn't allowed to put so much as a whisker inside the door.

## THE LOST SLIPPERS

'Now we can all have warm feet at night again!' cried Betty. 'You naughty little Spot! Wait till *you* have nice new slippers given to you! I'll run off with *yours*!'

'Woof!' said Spot. 'If you wait till *I* wear slippers, you'll wait a long time!'

Robina's Robins

# Robina's Robins

'I KNOW where my robins are nesting,' said Robina.

'You and your robins!' said Mummy. 'I suppose it's because of your name that you're so fond of robins! Where are they nesting?'

'I shan't tell *anyone*,' said Robina, 'in case somebody goes too near and frightens them off the nest, and makes them desert the young ones.'

'Oh, have they got young ones?' said Lennie. 'You *might* tell me, Robina – I promise I won't scare the parent birds.'

'No,' said Robina. 'I'm not telling *anyone*, so it's no good you asking, Lennie. But it's in a very,

very good place!'

Robina had two robins she liked very much. In the winter one had taken the east side of the garden for his own beat, and the other had taken the west side. They fought when they met halfway, and what a to-do there was then! Robina felt quite upset when she saw them flying round and about each other in the air, trying to peck feathers out of the other's neck!

They sometimes met on the bird table too, but they never fed there together. One waited till the other had finished, and then flew down. As Robina said, they simply would *not* be friends.

And then, one day in February, what a surprise! They sat on the bird table together, and were as friendly as could be, each pecking at the same boiled potato!

'Just *look*!' said Robina in surprise. 'What's happened to make them friends, Mummy?'

'Oh, I expect they've decided to get married and build a nest together,' said Mummy. And that is just what they did do! Robina was very pleased. She put out a small box on the bird table with bits of wool in it, and hairs from her brush, and dried moss and fluff from the carpet sweeper. The robins were very excited when they looked inside and saw all these.

They sang little trills to one another, and Robina said she knew what they were singing. 'They are singing "Just look here, my little dear, bits and pieces for our nest, I'll have all the moss and wool, and you can have the rest, *tirra-tirra-tirra-lee*!"'

That made Mummy and Lennie laugh. They looked out at the bird table – and certainly it did seem as if the robins were singing Robina's song to one another, *tirra-tirra-tirra-lee*!

She put out a little enamel bowl of water and each day they came to bathe in it together, splashing silvery drops all over the bird table. Then one day they discovered where Robina's bedroom was, and each morning they came on to a bough of the apple tree outside and sang to her.

'And do you know what they sing?' said Robina

to her mother. 'They sing, "Robina, we've seen her, Robina." Just like that! You listen, Mummy, and you'll hear them.'

'They do not,' said Lennie, quite jealous. But it really did sound like 'Robina, we've seen her, Robina!' trilled out in their rich, creamy voices.

Then one day Robina found their nest. It was on a shelf just inside the old potting shed at the bottom of the garden! She went in there one day to get a trowel, and just as she was looking for it she heard a tiny little trill. '*Tirra-lee!*'

'Why, that's one of my robins!' said Robina happily. 'Where are you, robin?'

'*Tirra-tirra-lee*,' answered the robin, and then Robina looked up to the topmost shelf, and saw a nest there, with a robin's perky little head looking out over the top!

'Oh, so *that's* where you're nesting!' said Robina in delight. 'I won't disturb you!'

Just then the second robin flew in at a crack in the

window. He had a wriggly grub in his mouth. His wife opened her beak and he popped it in.

'So you're sitting on eggs, are you, and your little mate is feeding you,' said Robina, pleased. 'Well, you can trust me, robins – I won't tell *anybody* where your nest is. Only Daddy and I come here – so if you keep quiet, even Daddy won't know anything about you. But he likes birds too, so if he sees you, don't be scared!'

One morning Robina was gardening not far from the little shed where the robins were when it began to rain. 'Blow!' said Robina. 'Now I shall have to go in! No, I won't, though. I'll just shelter in the robins' shed – the rain will soon blow over.'

So she went into the shed. She saw a small soft head look over the edge of the nest on the shelf. 'It's only me,' she said, and the robin was pleased. But then Robina noticed something. The rain was dripping through a leak in the roof, and splashing on to the robin's nest!

'Oh, dear – look at that!' said Robina. 'Your eggs must have hatched by now, and I expect you've got tiny baby birds in your nest, and you're keeping them warm. If you all get wet, the babies might die. But I daren't move your nest away from the drips, robin – you might be frightened and desert it!'

Soon the rain stopped, and the sun came out. The robin stood on the edge of the nest, looking very wet indeed. She had taken all the drips on her own little body, so that her nestlings might not get damp. She shook out her wings to dry them.

'Listen, robin – I think I know what has happened,' said Robina, and the tiny bird cocked her head on one side and listened. 'This shed is tiled, and I expect one of the tiles is loose. I'm sure I can put it right, if so. Don't be afraid if you hear me scrambling about on the shed roof.'

Robina went outside and looked up at the shed roof. Yes, one of the red tiles had slipped a little – and that was where the rain was leaking through, dripping on to the robins' nest.

She climbed up a nearby tree and then stepped down carefully on to the roof. She crawled up to where the loose tile was – but, alas, the roof was slippery with rain, and Robina suddenly found herself sliding down the tiles with nothing to catch hold of!

She fell right off the edge, and landed behind the shed, banging her head against the trunk of a tree as she fell. She lay where she had fallen, groaning a little, her eyes shut. Then she stopped groaning and lay still and silent.

The little robin who was out hunting for food for his young ones, saw her lying there when he came back with some greenfly in his beak. He was very surprised. He slipped in at the cracked window, and fed his young ones. Then he slipped out again and perched on a twig, looking down at Robina.

Why didn't she speak to him? He trilled his little song very gently, hoping that she would answer him in her soft voice. But she didn't! The robin hopped to a lower twig, and peered down at the little girl. He had never seen her with her eyes shut before, and he didn't like it. He went to tell his wife inside the shed, and she came to look at Robina too. They sang to one another in soft, low voices, which was their way of talking. Then the mother bird went back to her nest.

The little cock robin hopped down beside Robina's face and sang in her ear. But still she didn't say a word or look at him with big open eyes. He was frightened and worried. What was the matter with this big, kind friend of his?

He flew off to the house and saw Lennie working away at something by the open window. He stood on the sill and sang urgently. 'Robina, we've seen her, Robina!'

'Hallo,' said Lennie. 'I'm glad you've come to sing to *me* for a change! Mummy! Look at Robina's robin – he's singing like mad!'

'Where *is* Robina?' said Mummy. 'I haven't seen her all morning. She didn't come in for her eleven o'clock biscuits and milk. I hope she's all right. Call her, Lennie.'

Lennie shouted, but no Robina came. 'Go and look for her,' said Mummy. 'She's gardening somewhere.'

So Lennie went around the garden, but he couldn't see Robina anywhere, nor did she answer when he called. He didn't think of looking round the back of the old garden shed.

The robin followed him all the way. When Lennie came to the shed he sang very loudly indeed, and then when the boy didn't look round the back of shed he sang sadly and softly, and followed him all the way up the garden again.

'Robina's nowhere to be found,' said Lennie, worried. 'She doesn't answer to my shouts, and I can't see her *any*where!'

'But she *must* be in the garden!' said Mummy. 'Dear me, there's that robin of hers, singing its heart out on the windowsill again – and fluttering its wings – anyone would think it was worried too!'

'I think it is,' said Lennie, watching it. 'I believe it knows where Robina is, Mummy!' He went to the window, and the robin flew off a little way, singing loudly again, looking at Lennie all the time. 'I'm going to the robin,' said Lennie. 'You come, Mummy. It's trying to tell us something!'

So they both went out – and as soon as the robin saw them, he flew a little further down the garden, turning his head to them and singing loudly. When they were almost up to it again he flew off once more, to another tree.

'It's taking us somewhere,' said Mummy.

'Well, I don't know *where*!' said Lennie. 'I looked everywhere, Mummy!'

The robin took them right to the old shed, but he didn't go into it. Mummy and Lennie did, though, just to make sure that Robina wasn't there. She wasn't, of course. Then Mummy heard the robin outside, trilling so loudly that she was quite startled. 'Come quickly, Lennie,' she said, and ran out.

The robin was sitting on a branch of the tree that grew at the back of the shed. He sang again. 'Robina, we've seen her, Robina!'

Yes. There *was* Robina, lying still and quiet under the tree at the back of the shed!

Mummy knelt down beside her. 'Robina! Darling!' she said. 'What happened?'

And Robina slowly opened her eyes! She tried to sit up, but her head swam and she couldn't. The little robin in the tree above sang loudly again. He was so pleased to see Robina's eyes once more. He hadn't liked them to be shut. He wished she would speak.

She did. 'Oh, Mummy, where am I? Oh, I remember now – I fell off the shed roof and bumped my head!'

'Lennie – go and fetch Daddy,' said Mummy. 'He must carry Robina indoors.'

'I can walk all right,' said Robina, but Mummy wouldn't let her. In half a minute Daddy came running down, and very soon he was carrying Robina into the house. The robin followed, anxious to see that his friend was all right. He flew to her bedroom windowsill and watched her mother undressing her and popping her into bed.

'You must rest for a day or two,' she said. 'You have a terrible bump on your poor old head, Robina. To think you climbed on that slippery roof to stop the rain from pouring on to your robins! Well, it was the little cock robin who came to tell us where you were!'

'*Was* it?' said Robina, delighted. 'Oh, look – he's on the windowsill now, peering in. I can hear him singing. Listen!'

So he was – his favourite song too: 'Robina, we've seen her, Robina!'

Tomorrow she is going to have a surprise. The two robins are going to bring their young ones to see Robina! They can all fly now, and are the prettiest little things.

Won't Robina be delighted to see them all on her windowsill? *I'd* like to see them too.

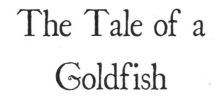

# The Tale of a Goldfish

# The Tale of a Goldfish

THERE WAS once a small goldfish who swam round and round in a bowl. He was a pretty little fellow, and when he was first put in the bowl he felt very merry and bright.

He had been in an enormous tank with hundreds of other goldfish, and it had been fun swimming here and there with big and tiny fish. There had been plenty of friends to play about with, and it was fun to chase one another round the tank.

He belonged now to a little girl called Mary. She had no pets at all, so she was excited when her granny gave her a goldfish for her birthday in a jar.

'Here is the money to buy him a bowl to swim in,' said Granny, and Mary went off proudly to buy a nice little home for her pet.

The money didn't buy a *very* big bowl, and the goldfish soon grew tired of swimming round and round it with no one to play with him. His pretty fins drooped, and he stayed still in the bowl instead of swimming round fast.

Mary wondered what was the matter with him. 'Do you think he's lonely?' she asked her mother. 'Do you think he's bored?'

'Well, yes, I do,' said Mummy. 'After all, most fish have an interesting life in a pond, where they can swim in and out of water weed, and pass the time of day with a snail or two and other fish.'

'I hope he's not going to die,' said Mary anxiously. 'Mummy, you know that pond over by the mill? It's full of water weed – could I go and get some? He might like that. He could swim in and out of it then.'

'Yes. That's a good idea!' said her mother. 'Also,

water weed would help to keep the water pure. It sends up little bubbles all the time, you know, Mary – we wouldn't have to change the water so often if we had water weed growing in it.'

Daddy came in just then and looked at the drooping little fish. 'Perhaps he's got a chill,' he said. 'When did you change the water, Mary?'

'Yesterday,' said Mary. 'It got so thick and horrid.'

'Did you make sure that the new water was as warm as the old?' asked Daddy. 'You see, the water in the bowl gets warm when it's in here – but the water from the cold tap is very chilly.'

'Oh! I never thought of that!' said Mary. 'Poor little fish! I gave him water straight from the cold tap – and I could so easily have added a little warm water to it! I expect he's got a chill!'

'Well, if you have a pet, you must take great care of it and cherish it,' said Daddy. 'After all, a pet depends on its owner for everything – whether it's a horse, a dog, or a little goldfish! We'll have to do something to make your fish happy and well again!'

'Let's go to the pond and get some weed, Daddy,' said Mary. 'And we might find a little snail or two to keep him company. Would he like that, do you think?'

'Oh, yes, and as he can't eat the snail and the snail can't do him any harm they will be quite good friends,' said Daddy.

So Daddy and Mary set off after their dinner, and went to the small pond over by the old mill. It was a quiet little place, with two or three kinds of weed growing in it.

Mary bent over the water. 'There are plenty of snails, Daddy,' she said. 'Different shapes too. Look, there's one with a long thin spiral shell – and here's a dear little coiled one. Shall we have one of each kind?'

'Oh, we'll take half a dozen,' said Daddy. 'And plenty of weed. We'll take more than we want and put the extra into a pail, so that if the weed in the bowl dies, we shall have plenty of fresh weed to hand.'

Mary saw something moving very slowly at the bottom of the muddy pond. She put in her hand and scooped out a funny little creature, encased in a tube-like shell.

'Look, Daddy!' she said, surprised. 'Is *this* a snail too? It's quite different from the other snails we have.'

'No. That's a caddis grub,' said Daddy. 'He has a soft little body, so he makes himself a hard tube to keep his body safe! He can put out his head, look, and can crawl about in the mud, but he can hide his head in his case when an enemy comes near! He will one day grow wings and fly away – a little caddis moth!'

'Oh! He'll be quite safe with the goldfish then, won't he?' said Mary. 'Let's go back now, Daddy, and give him the weed, and the snails and caddis grub for company.'

'We'll empty some of the pond water into his bowl too,' said her daddy. 'It may contain tiny water creatures that the goldfish will like as a change of food. Come along.'

So home they went, and soon the goldfish bowl looked a very different place! It had three or four strands of different weed floating about, and quite a number of snails crawling here and there – and the funny little caddis grub!

The goldfish was most excited. His fins spread out, he swam round merrily and he went to look at every snail in his bowl.

'He's making friends!' said Mary. 'Oh, isn't he happy now, Daddy? I wish I could tell everyone how to make their goldfish happy, if he has only a bowl to swim in!'

Well, *I've* told you, haven't I?

# The New Little
# Milkman

# The New Little
# Milkman

THERE WAS once a little boy whose father had six cows. He sold the milk that the cows gave him, and made quite a lot of money. He had a small black pony and a neat milk cart that took the milk round to all his customers.

Now Freddy, the little boy, often used to go round with his father and the pony. It was fun to give out the milk to old Mrs Lacy, and young Mrs Thomas, and Mr Timms and all the rest. Freddy knew all the customers, and said 'Good morning' to them in just the same cheerful voice as his father's.

Somebody else often used to go in the milk cart too

– and that somebody was Tommy, the big puppy dog. He belonged to Freddy, and he was such a big clumsy thing, so loving and happy. Freddy loved him very much indeed.

Freddy made himself a little milk cart from a big wooden box. His father put some wheels on it and a shelf all the way round for milk bottles. The bottles were only toy bricks, of course, because his father wouldn't give him real bottles.

Freddy had to be the horse and the milkman too.

'I'm the galloping horse!' he told Tommy, and he stamped his foot on the ground. 'I'm taking the milk round. Hear me go clip-clop, clip-clop. Now here I am at old Mrs Lacy's. Now I'm the milkman. Good morning, Mrs Lacy. A pint of milk today? Here it is. Thank you. What a fine morning it is!'

Then he took hold of the handles of his wooden cart and was the pony again. Tommy watched him and thought that Freddy was wonderful.

Then one morning a great idea came into Tommy's

head. Why shouldn't *he* be the horse? Couldn't he pull the cart for Freddy? Of course! And then Freddy could be the milkman and stay at the back of the cart instead of sometimes being the horse and sometimes the milkman.

So the next time that Freddy played at being the milkman, Tommy ran to the cart and put himself between the two long handles.

Freddy gave a shout when he saw him. 'Tommy! You're the cleverest dog in the world! You really are. I can see you want to be the horse. All right, you shall be! I'll get a rope for reins, and tie you in properly.'

So before long Tommy was harnessed to the wooden milk cart, and the two of them went round the garden together, stopping whenever Freddy said he had come to somebody who wanted milk.

'Mr Timms! How much milk today? Good morning to you! Mrs Jenks? I'm sorry, I've no cream at all. I'll have some eggs tomorrow.'

It was a good game to play. Tommy and Freddy never got tired of it. Sometimes they both went in the real milk cart, and then the two of them watched and remembered every single customer, so that they might play the game properly.

One day something horrid happened. Freddy's father went out with his pony and milk cart on a very frosty day. The roads were slippery, and as they went up High Hill the little black pony slipped and fell. The milkman ran to help her up, and she kicked out as she tried to rise.

Quite by accident she kicked Freddy's father on the leg. Poor man! *He* fell down then, and a passersby had to come and pick him up. His leg was badly hurt – and the poor little pony had a hurt leg too.

'Well, this *is* an upset!' said Freddy's mother, when the milkman was carried home, and the little black pony was back in her shed, having limped all the way home with the milk cart. 'What a good thing you had delivered all your milk!'

'Maybe we shall both be better tomorrow,' said the milkman, lying back in bed. 'You can milk the cows, can't you, my dear? Freddy can help. He's a good little lad. See to the pony for me, and get the doctor to him too, if he needs it.'

Well, the animal doctor said that the pony was not to walk for a week, or he would be lame for the rest of his life. And the milkman's doctor said that he too must lie in bed for a week or more, or *his* leg would not get better either.

'And *now* what are we to do?' said Freddy's mother to Freddy. 'I could take the milk round myself in the cart if only the pony was all right. But I can't possibly carry all that milk myself. Besides, I don't know the customers.'

Freddy stared at his mother and his heart began to beat fast. He had thought of a perfectly wonderful idea.

'Mother! You and I will milk the cows and bottle the milk,' said the little boy. 'And then *I* will take the milk round in my little wooden milk cart.

'Oh, Freddy dear, don't be silly!' said his mother. 'You can't drag all that milk round by yourself.'

'I'm not going to,' said Freddy. 'Tommy can do that. You've seen him playing at being my pony, haven't you, Mother?'

'Well, I never! What ideas you do get!' said his mother, laughing. 'And do you really suppose you could get all the milk bottles into that little cart of yours, Freddy?'

'No, I couldn't,' said Freddy. 'But I could keep coming back for more.'

'But you don't know all the houses where Daddy takes his milk!' said his mother.

'Yes, I do,' said Freddy. 'I've often been with Daddy and I know everybody. Really I do, Mother. Do let me try.'

'Well, I really don't see how we are going to get the milk round,' said his mother. 'I'll let you try. Freddy, just take a few of the most important people their milk. There's Mrs Thomas, with her five children –

she really *must* have her milk. And there's old Mr Harris. He's ill and has to have lots of milk too. You must take his as well.'

Well, you can't imagine how excited Freddy felt! He ran to tell Tommy.

'Tommy! Just fancy! Our game of pretend is going to be REAL!' cried Freddy. 'What do you think of that?'

Tommy wagged his big tail and jumped around in glee. He was always pleased when Freddy was happy.

The cows were milked the next morning. The milk was put into clean bottles – big bottles and little bottles. Then Freddy ran to get his cart. He carefully put the bottles into it. He could only get fifteen in, but that didn't matter. He could easily come back for more!

Then he harnessed Tommy to the wooden milk cart. Tommy was pleased to be a real pony this time, with real, heavy milk bottles to pull along instead of wooden bricks.

'Goodbye, Mother, we're going!' shouted Freddy.

And off they went. Tommy clattered out of the farmyard with the wooden cart behind him, and Freddy ran behind the cart, clicking to Tommy as if he were a real horse.

They stopped at Mrs Lacy's. She opened the door, surprised. 'Why, I thought there would be no milk this morning!' she said. 'I heard about the accident. Dear me, what a marvellous boy you are to be sure! You've got a milk cart and dog-pony of your own! I'll have a pint of milk, please. Here's the money. And tell your mother from me that she's got a fine, helpful little boy!'

Freddy grinned happily. He put the money into a bag. Then he set off for the next customer, Mrs Thomas. She was waiting for him anxiously.

'Oh, Freddy! I was so afraid I would get no milk for all my children this morning!' she said. 'What a good boy you are! And I do like your horse and cart. I must find a biscuit for the horse.'

She gave Tommy a biscuit and he munched it up at

once, wagging his tail so hard that he almost knocked a bottle over in the cart. Freddy was given a chocolate and the money for the milk.

He went on to the other customers. He knew them all, and didn't miss a single one out. He had to go back home three times to fill up his cart again with bottles of milk. He sold it all, and took his mother the money.

She counted it out. 'Exactly right!' she said. 'Well, I never knew before what a sensible, clever little boy you are, Freddy! And as for Tommy he's a treasure! I'll give him a bone at once!'

So Tommy had an extra-large bone, and Freddy had a big piece of ginger cake and two peppermints. He went to see his father and told him all about the morning.

'Thank you, Freddy. You *are* a help!' said his father. 'I was afraid I should lose all my customers this week, but I see I shan't. You and Tommy are fine.'

Well, Freddy and Tommy worked very hard all

that week until the milkman and the little black pony were both better. Then, the next Tuesday, the pony was put into the real milk cart again, and the milkman himself drove off with all his bottles of creamy milk.

'I'm quite sad that we're not the milkman and his horse any more,' Freddy told his mother.

She smiled at him. 'Well, you can be my errand boy now,' she said. 'I want to buy a few presents for a kind little boy I know. Will you go and choose them? Take your cart with you, and ask Tommy to pull them all home for you. I want you to buy a packet of chocolate, a bottle of sweets, a new kite and a storybook. Here's the money.'

'Who are the presents for?' asked Freddy, astonished. 'Is somebody having a birthday?'

'No,' said his mother. 'The presents are for *you*, of course! Daddy and I are very grateful to you for your help, you see, and we want to give you a reward. Oh, I've forgotten something. Buy a new ball for Tommy too. Now off you go!'

So off went the two of them as happy as could be. And what a time Freddy had choosing all the things and bringing them home in his cart. But he did deserve them, didn't he?

# Go Away, Black Cat!

THE BLACK cat was a great nuisance in the nursery. He wasn't very large and he didn't make any noise – but he would keep getting out the farmyard animals and playing with them!

He sent them sliding all around the floor with his paw, and then pounced after them. The animals were made of wood, so he couldn't really hurt them, but they didn't like being slid all over the place like that.

'Go away, black cat!' said the pink pig from the farmyard.

'Go away, black cat!' mooed the cow, who was a little bit afraid of having her long tail broken.

'Oh, go away, black cat!' scolded the sheep, who was very tired of being pushed all over the room just to please the cat.

The black cat said nothing. He didn't even 'miaow'. He only came in because he loved to play with the little toys and send them hopping about the room. It was fun to hear them shouting at him too and not take any notice.

'I wish we could stop him!' said the toy farmer, who was always afraid he might be sent sliding over the floor too. He usually hurried into his farmhouse when he saw the black cat, but he knew quite well that the cat could put his paw into the farmhouse and get him out if he wished!

'I know, I know what we can do!' squeaked a tiny little doll dressed as a sailor. He sat in a small wooden boat, and was cross because the others didn't take much notice of him.

'Oh, you be quiet,' said the bear. 'You're always talking.'

'But I know what to do!' cried the sailor doll.

'No, you don't,' the toy rabbit said rudely. 'Be quiet! How could a tiny thing like you know better than big toys like us?'

The sailor doll sulked and said no more.

The red-haired doll thought it would be a good idea to let the three toy dogs bark at the black cat and frighten him. So the black dog, the white dog and the pink dog were all arranged in a row in front of the farmyard, ready to bark.

How they barked when the black cat appeared! 'Woof, woof! Go away, black cat! Woof, woof! Go away, black cat!'

The black cat looked at them and grinned till his mouth nearly reached his ears. Then he began to play with the toy dogs! He sent them here and he sent them there; he threw them into the air – he had a lovely time!

But the dogs didn't. They were very angry. When the black cat had gone the tiny sailor doll spoke again.

'I know what to do. I know what—'

'Be quiet!' shouted the bear. 'Toys, I've got a fine idea! Let's stand by the door with a pail of water and empty it over the cat when he comes in!'

So they filled a little seaside pail with water and waited by the door. But the black cat jumped in at the window, and when he saw the bear and the rabbit waiting with their pail of water he ran to them and tipped up the pail so that the water wet their feet! Then he played with the farmyard animals and broke the leg of one of the pigs.

The sailor doll didn't say any more. He went to the Noah's ark and lifted up the lid. 'Noah!' he said. 'Take your animals for a walk round the room. It will do them good.'

So Noah took all his animals two by two round the room, and the sailor doll waited patiently by the ark. Soon the black cat peeped in at the door, and the sailor doll began to behave in a very peculiar manner.

He began to scrape inside the ark as if he had gone

mad, and he shouted out, 'A mouse! A mouse! You naughty mouse, come out of the ark! You have frightened away Noah and all his animals!'

The black cat pricked up his ears at the word 'mouse'. He saw Noah and the animals walking round the room, and he sprang to the ark to find the mouse.

'Get in and catch it! Get in and catch it!' cried the sailor doll, and the cat jumped right inside the big wooden ark.

Slam! The sailor doll shut down the lid with a bang, and yelled to the other toys, 'Come and help me. Put something on top, quick! Come and put something on top!'

They all rushed to the ark, carrying many different things. The rabbit carried a stool. The red-haired doll carried a big top. The bear brought two books. Everybody brought something.

Bang! Bang! Bang! Everything was slammed down on to the lid of the ark. More books were fetched, and somehow or other the rabbit and the bear eventually managed to balance the sailor doll's little wooden boat on the Noah's ark too to keep down the lid.

The black cat banged his head against the lid trying to get out. He had seen at once that there was no mouse there, and now he was frightened. Suppose he never got out of this dreadful dark wooden place that smelt of the Noah's ark animals!

'Let-me-*ow*-out!' he mewed. 'Let-me-*ow*-out!'

'Well, do you promise never, never to come into our room again?' cried the sailor doll boldly. 'If you do come again, I'll lock you into a brick box and put it at the bottom of the cupboard where nobody will find it!'

'Oh, *ow*! Oh, *ow*!' wailed the black cat. 'Don't do that! I'll never, never come here again! Let-me-*ow*-out!'

The sailor doll chuckled to himself. He cried out loudly, 'Well – one, two, three – out you come!' He upset all the things on the lid and they crashed to the floor. The black cat lifted up the lid with his head and jumped out.

He tore out of the room at top speed, yowling loudly. The sailor doll chuckled. 'You can come back, Noah!' he shouted to Noah and the animals. Then he turned to the watching toys, who all looked pleased and astonished.

'Now maybe you see that you should listen to me whenever I begin to talk!' he said. 'Do you understand?'

'Yes, Sailor Doll!' answered all the toys most politely. And now I expect that the sailor doll will talk all day long, don't you?

# Pippitty's Pet Canary

# Pippitty's Pet Canary

LITTLE PRINCESS Pippitty had a beautiful yellow canary called Goldie. She loved it very much, and looked after it every day. She loved it far better than any of her other pets, and when the king and queen took her away to the seaside for a holiday she wanted to take Goldie too.

'No, you can't do that,' said the queen. 'Goldie must stay behind with all your dogs and cats and ponies. We will ask Gobbo the elf to look after Goldie for you.'

'But suppose he lets Goldie fly away!' cried Pippitty. 'It would break my heart, really it would.'

'Well, if he lets your canary escape, he will lose his head!' said the king. 'Now cheer up, Pippitty – you may be sure Gobbo doesn't want his head cut off, and he will look after Goldie very well indeed.'

The day came for the king and queen and Pippitty to start off in the golden coach. Pippitty said goodbye to all her pets, and kissed her canary on his little yellow beak.

'See that you look after Goldie well, Gobbo,' said the king. 'Feed him every day, give him fresh water to drink and to bathe in and clean out his cage – and whatever you do, don't let him fly away! If you let him escape, off will come your head!'

'I will look after him well,' promised Gobbo, and he bowed very low. Then the princess blew a last kiss to her canary and stepped into the golden coach. Off they all went to the seaside.

Gobbo went to the canary's cage every day and did all that he had been told to do. Goldie fretted for the princess and sat all day long on his perch, moping.

Gobbo tried to cheer him up, but it was no use.

'Where's the princess?' Goldie kept asking. 'Where's Pippitty? Let me out, Gobbo, and I will go and look for her.'

'Oh, no, I mustn't let you out,' said Gobbo. 'Be patient, Goldie. Pippitty will be back soon. I should lose my head if I let you out of your cage.'

The time went by, and at last came the day when the princess Pippitty was to come back home again. Gobbo went to Goldie's cage and cleaned it out beautifully. Then he polished the bars till they shone like gold.

'You haven't given me enough water to bathe in,' complained Goldie. 'I shall tell Pippitty when she comes back.'

'Pippitty is coming back today,' said Gobbo.

'Oh, I don't believe you!' said the canary. 'You have kept saying she would be back soon, she would be back soon, and she didn't come. Give me some more water to bathe in.'

Gobbo opened the door of the cage, and he was just

going to put some more water in when someone at the door called, 'Gobbo! Gobbo! Come quickly and see the rainbow!'

Gobbo put the water down quickly and ran to the window – and, alas, he forgot to shut the cage door! In a trice Goldie was out of the cage and flying round the room. Gobbo shut the window with a bang, and then ran to shut the door. The canary could not get out of the room.

Gobbo's friend, Peepo, the one who had told him to look at the rainbow, stared at Gobbo in surprise.

'What are you shutting the doors and windows for?' he asked. 'Do you feel cold?'

'No,' said Gobbo, 'but don't you see that Goldie the canary has escaped? I shall lose my head if the princess comes back and sees him out of his cage.'

'Oh, my, oh, my!' said Peepo in dismay. 'Do go back to your cage, Goldie.'

'Not I!' said Goldie. 'Once out of my cage I'll never go back! I'll just wait till the princess comes and then I'll fly down to her shoulder and ask her to let me be free.'

'You wouldn't be safe if you flew out of doors like the other birds,' said Gobbo. 'You don't know how to find your own food. Be a sensible little bird and go back to your beautiful big cage.'

But Goldie wouldn't. Gobbo began to cry, for he felt quite certain that his head would be cut off when the king and queen returned. Peepo sighed in despair, for he knew that if only he hadn't called Gobbo to look at the rainbow, his friend wouldn't have let the canary escape.

Suddenly there came a knock at the door and in came Merry-one the jester. The canary flew to the door to get out, but Merry-one shut it just in time.

'Hallo, hallo!' he said in surprise. 'What's this I see? Goldie out of his cage! I fear you will lose your head for this, Gobbo.'

'Oh, Merry-one, help me to get Goldie back!' begged Gobbo, the tears running down his cheeks.

'How did he get out?' asked Merry-one.

'Well, you see,' said Gobbo, 'I was just giving Goldie some more water when Peepo called out to me to go and see the rainbow, and while I was looking Goldie—'

'Wait a minute, wait a minute!' said Merry-one, looking puzzled. 'I'm getting muddled. Now, let's begin again. Goldie was giving Peepo some water, and you saw a rainbow?'

'No, no,' said Gobbo. '*I* was giving Goldie some water, and Peepo called out—'

'Where was Peepo?' asked Merry-one, looking more puzzled than ever. 'Was he in the cage?'

'No, *I* was in the cage, you silly creature!' cried the canary.

'Oh, *you* were in the cage,' said Merry-one. 'Well, Peepo was giving you some water, and Gobbo called out to him to see a rainbow, and—'

'No, no, *no*!' said Gobbo and Peepo together. 'You've got it all wrong.'

'You *are* a foolish fellow!' said the canary, fluttering his wings crossly, 'Begin at the beginning now. I was in the cage.'

'Yes,' said Merry-one. 'I was in the cage – no, no, that's wrong, of course. Gobbo was in the cage, and Goldie was – no, that's wrong too. Oh, my, I'm getting so muddled, I shall never, never understand this!'

'I'll *make* you understand!' cried the canary in a rage. 'Look here, you foolish fellow. *I* was in the cage – like this –' and Goldie flew back into his cage, and stood on the perch. 'Do you understand that, Merry-one?'

'Perfectly, thank you!' cried the jester, and he banged the cage door shut. '*You* were in the cage, Goldie, ha, ha! And you are in the cage now! Ho, ho! Oh, yes, I understand all right and so do the others, I'm sure!'

'Ha, ha!' roared Gobbo and Peepo joyfully. 'Oh, Merry-one, we thought you were being so silly, and really you were as clever as could be!'

'Oh, thank you, thank you for saving my head for me!' said Gobbo, and he shook Merry-one gratefully by the hand.

Goldie the canary flew into a terrible rage and shook the bars of his cage till they rattled – but nobody took any notice. They had heard the sound of cheering outside.

'The princess! The king and queen!' cried Peepo and Gobbo, and they rushed to the window. Sure enough, there was the golden coach, and, as the three watched, the king and the queen stepped out, and little Princess Pippitty followed.

And the very first thing she did was to rush upstairs to see Goldie her canary! Wasn't it a good thing he was safely back in his cage? He was so delighted to see Pippitty that he forgot all about his bad temper, and sang her a beautiful song of welcome.

Nobody told tales of Gobbo, so his head was quite safe – but, dear me, didn't he have a narrow escape?

# The Foolish
# Guinea Pig

# The Foolish Guinea Pig

TUBBY THE guinea pig lived in a small hutch in the garden all by himself. He was a fat and foolish little creature, and everyone laughed at him. He was very happy, for he had plenty of food to eat and a kind girl for a mistress – but there was one thing he always grumbled about.

He had never been asked to a party!

He saw the rabbits in the fields having parties and playing games together. He saw the birds crowding together and having fine fun at a bird-table party. He saw the pixies at night hurrying off in their best clothes to a dance. But nobody ever asked Tubby to a party.

He made up a little song about it:

> *I'm a guinea pig, fat and hearty,*
> *And I'd love to go to a party,*
> *But* nobody *sends me a card to say,*
> *Please come to supper with me today!*

He sang this song whenever anyone came by, and one day Reynard the fox heard him and came to have a look into his cage. When he saw the fat little guinea pig he licked his lips.

'So you want to go to a party, do you?' he said to Tubby. 'Well, so you shall! It's a shame that you have never been asked! I am giving a party on Saturday night, and am asking four of my special friends. I will send you an invitation card too.'

Well, Tubby was too excited for words! He squeaked with joy all that day and told everyone that came by.

Woffle-nose the bunny scampered near, and Tubby

called to him. 'Woffle-nose! I'm going to the fox's party on Saturday. Have you been asked too?'

'I should hope not!' said Woffle-nose and scurried away.

A big cock pheasant flew down and pecked up some seeds nearby, and Tubby called to him. 'I'm going to the fox's party on Saturday. Have you been asked too?'

'I should hope not!' said the pheasant and flew off.

Then four little pixies came running by, and Tubby called to them too. 'Pixies! I'm going to the fox's party on Saturday. Have you been asked too?'

'We should hope not!' said the pixies and hurried away.

'Now why have none of them been asked, and why do they hope they won't be?' wondered foolish Tubby. 'A party is a lovely thing – plenty to eat, and lots of fun.'

Prickles the hedgehog came scuffling by on his short legs. Tubby called to him. 'Prickles! I'm going to the fox's party on Saturday. Have you been asked too?'

'Of course not!' said Prickles. 'And if you are wise, you won't go, Tubby! The fox wants *you* for his dinner!'

'Oh, I don't believe that!' said Tubby at once. 'The fox was most polite to me. He is asking four other friends too – he can't be going to eat them all! I shall be quite safe.'

'Now listen to me,' said Prickles. 'I have a little plan. My hole is near the entrance to the fox's earth. Come to it half an hour before the time you have been asked for the party, and you can peep out of it and see who the other party people are. If you like the look of them, you can brush your whiskers with my brush and go. If not, you can lie hidden.'

'Very well,' said Tubby. 'But of course I shall go! I'm not going to miss my first party!'

Half an hour before the time that Tubby was asked to the party, he turned up at Prickles's hole. The hedgehog let him squeeze in beside him, and then they both lay down and watched.

Before long there came the sound of pattering feet, and Tubby looked out, his head hidden by a fern. He saw a large fox going down the entrance to the fox's den.

'That's Sharp-tooth,' whispered Prickles. 'He must be one of the guests. Here's another.'

Tubby saw yet another fox. 'That's Crunch-you-up!' whispered Prickles. 'And look – here are two foxes together, Grab-you and Snap-Snap. See their great teeth!'

Tubby did see them, and he began to tremble. So these were the other guests. He didn't like the look of them at all. And yet – oh, he did so badly want to go to a party!

Soon the first fox came to the entrance of the hole and sniffed. 'Tubby isn't anywhere in sight!' he called down the hole to his guests. 'How late he is! Well, so long as he is fat, who cares! He will make a fine pie. I've got the dish all ready and the crust is made.'

Well! Poor Tubby shivered and shook so much with fright that Prickles thought he must be turning into a jelly.

'Don't worry!' he said. 'I'll take you safely home tonight, Tubby.'

He did – after the foxes had waited and waited, and then gone home grumbling savagely. How pleased Tubby was to be safely in his little cage again, the door tightly shut. He was just falling asleep when he heard a sharp bark nearby and saw the nose of Reynard the fox peeping in at him.

'You were not able to come to our party, I see,' said the fox politely. 'Well, never mind. We had a good time, and we hope to see you at the next one – Saturday night, Tubby, so don't forget.'

'I shan't forget, and I shan't be there,' said Tubby. 'I'm not the little silly you take me for, Reynard!'

But he nearly was, wasn't he? He doesn't want to go to parties now, and has quite forgotten the sad little song he made up. Prickles the hedgehog is his best friend, and they have good times together – but no parties for Tubby! He shakes like a jelly if you even *mention* the word.

# The Dog Without
## a Collar

# The Dog Without a Collar

BOBBO WAS a fat little puppy, and he belonged to Rosie who loved him very much. When he was six months old Rosie's father said that he must now have a collar with his name and address on it. So Rosie took him to a pet shop with her mother, and together they chose a beautiful red collar for him.

'We will have his name and address on a little silver tag to hang on to his collar,' said Mother. The shop assistant showed Mother and Rosie some round silver tags, and they chose the one they liked best.

'Please put Bobbo's name and address on by the time we come back from our walk,' said Mother. Sure enough, when they called at the shop again the collar was ready, and neatly printed on the little round tag was:

BOBBO,

C/O ROSIE BROWN

HIGH STREET,

BENTON

'Oh, doesn't it look nice!' said Rosie, pleased. 'Won't Bobbo be proud to have a brand-new collar of his own?' But Bobbo wasn't at all proud or pleased!

When Rosie buckled it round his neck he wriggled and struggled to get away, and was as naughty as could be.

'Oh, Bobbo!' said Rosie, disappointed. 'Why don't you like your lovely red collar? All dogs wear them, and, see, I have had your name and address put on this little round tag for you.'

But Bobbo yelped and barked crossly, and when at last the collar was on he did his best to bite it – but, of course, he couldn't because it was round his neck.

'You shall only wear it when we go out, till you get used to it, if it bothers you,' said Rosie kindly. So each night she took it off and popped it into a drawer.

One night she forgot to put it into the drawer. She left it on the chair instead. Bobbo saw it, and when he was alone he went up to it and snarled.

'You horrid thing!' he said. 'You nasty collar! I've a good mind to chew you!'

He took it into his mouth and bit it hard. Then he heard someone coming, and he quickly ran into the kitchen with the collar and dropped it into a bucket under the sink. Wasn't it naughty of him? He thought no one would find it there.

Next morning Rosie looked everywhere for Bobbo's collar, but it was nowhere to be seen. Bobbo lay in his basket and said nothing. He was feeling very pleased to think that he wouldn't be able to wear that horrible collar all day.

Father found it when he took the bucket to fill

with water. 'Rosie, Rosie!' he cried. 'Here is Bobbo's collar. It was in my bucket.'

'Well, however could it have got there?' said Rosie in surprise. 'Bobbo, come here! I'll put it round your neck!'

Bobbo was angry. He made up his mind to bury his collar in the garden, where no one could find it, the next time he could get hold of it.

Two days later, as he was playing about the garden his collar came off all by itself! Rosie hadn't buckled it properly, and it had come undone. Bobbo was delighted.

'Woof!' he barked. 'Now I'll bury it deep down in the earth where no one will ever be able to find it again!'

He dug a big hole, dropped the collar down into it and then covered it over with earth. How pleased he was!

*Now I'll go out for a walk by myself without a collar*, he thought. *How jealous all the other dogs will be to see me without a collar!*

Off he went. He walked down the street with his head well up in the air, and when he met another dog he woofed loudly.

'Woof!' he said. 'Why do you bother to wear a collar? I don't!'

'You'll wish you did sooner or later,' said the dog scornfully. 'You're silly.'

The next dog he met laughed at him. 'Only puppies don't wear collars,' he said. 'I suppose you're a silly puppy still?'

Bobbo went on and on – and when he had gone a very long way indeed, and had turned his nose up at quite twenty dogs with collars, he thought it was time to go home again. But oh my goodness me! He didn't know the way back! He had been so busy making faces at the dogs he met that he hadn't noticed the way he had come. He felt very much afraid.

'Oh, dear!' he said, looking all around. 'I wonder which is the right way to go?'

He chose a road that looked like one he knew – but

it was the wrong one, and soon poor Bobbo found himself further still from his home. He yelped in fear and wondered what he should do. He saw a garden gate standing open and he went into the garden to see if there was anything to eat there, for he really was getting very hungry.

Suddenly he heard an angry voice shouting at him. 'You bad dog! What are you doing in my garden? No dogs are allowed here. Go away! Look what a mess you've made of my wallflowers, scraping up the earth like that!'

Bobbo looked up and saw an old woman shaking her fist at him angrily. He forgot where the gate was and tore off towards the house. He ran into the hall, and the old woman ran after him.

'Come out! Come out!' she shouted. 'Oh, look at your muddy paw marks all over my clean hall! You bad, naughty dog! Just wait till I see who you belong to and then I'll tell your master just how very bad you've been!'

Bobbo felt himself caught, and he stood trembling to see what would happen. He felt the old woman's fingers round his neck, and then she said in surprise, 'Why, you haven't got a collar on, so I can't see your name and address. I shall have to call a policeman and tell him you're a stray dog.'

Oh, dear! Call a policeman! Poor Bobbo shook all over. He didn't want to go to prison, and he thought he might have to for making a mess of the old lady's clean hall.

The old woman went into the garden and looked over the gate. She knew that a policeman came down her street about that time. She saw him and called to him. Bobbo saw him walk up to the gate and he tried to hide himself, but it wasn't a bit of use.

'There's a stray dog here, constable,' said the old woman. 'He's got no collar on and no name or address, and he's made a dreadful mess of my garden and hall. You'd better take him along to the police station.'

'Very good, madam,' said the policeman, and he

picked Bobbo up and carried him away. Poor Bobbo! How he shivered and shook with fright! He soon arrived at the police station, and another policeman looked at him sternly and wrote something down in a book.

'Why don't people put collars on their dogs with their names and addresses?' said the second policeman crossly. 'It's such a waste of time, having to keep dogs here.'

Bobbo was put into a bare little room by himself. He was hungry and thirsty, but the policemen were far too busy to think about the dog just then. So Bobbo lay down on the floor to see what would happen next.

Nothing happened. The policemen forgot all about him, and the evening came. It grew dark in the little bare room, and poor Bobbo was cold and frightened.

'Oh, if only I'd got my red collar on!' he whined. 'Then the policemen would know my name and where I lived and they would take me home. But they don't know who I am, and Rosie doesn't know where to look for me, and I can't find my way home even if I could escape, which I can't. Oh, why was I silly enough to bury my beautiful collar? All dogs wear collars, they are nice things to have. I do want my collar again!'

Suddenly the telephone rang, making Bobbo jump terribly. He heard the policeman in the next room answering it, and his heart jumped for joy when he heard what was said.

'Hallo, hallo,' said the policeman. 'This is the police station . . . Yes, we do happen to have a stray dog here, a puppy. But he's got no collar on, so we couldn't take him home . . . Yes, he's black and white and very fat . . . Very well, miss, I'll keep him till you come for him.'

Bobbo guessed that Rosie must have telephoned the police station about him when he didn't come in for his tea. He was so glad to think that he wouldn't have to go to prison, but was going home instead that he frisked round and round the little bare room for joy.

Soon the door opened – and in came Rosie and her

mother! You should have seen Bobbo rush to them! He jumped into the air, he licked their hands, he barked for joy. And all the time he was trying to say, 'I'm very sorry I hid my collar. I'll dig it up again and wear it tomorrow like a good dog!'

But Rosie and her mother didn't understand what he was saying. They just kissed him and hugged him, and then carried him home. They gave him some hot bread and milk as soon as they were home, and then he curled up in his basket and fell fast asleep, tired out after all his adventures. Next morning when Rosie called him he ran up to her.

'I've got to get some more money out of my money box to pay for a new collar for you,' said Rosie. 'I don't know where your other one is. You are costing me a lot of money, Bobbo dear, because I had to give the policeman five whole pounds for being kind enough to look after you when you were lost yesterday. I do wish you hadn't lost your collar. If you had had it on, you would have been brought home as soon as you were lost, instead of having to go to the police station!'

Bobbo listened with his head on one side. He felt very much ashamed of himself. He ran to the garden and dug quickly where he had buried his collar. Soon he had found it, and he carried it in his mouth to Rosie and put it down at her feet.

She was surprised. 'Oh, Bobbo, you buried it!' she said. 'Well, you have had your punishment, so I won't scold you any more. But I hope you will be a good dog in future and wear your collar every day without making a fuss.'

Bobbo let Rosie put it round his neck. Then he licked her hand and barked. 'I'll be a good dog now and always wear my collar!' he said.

He kept his word and Rosie never had to look for his collar ever again, because it was always round his neck, making him look very neat and smart.

What an adventure he had, didn't he?

# The Cat Who Cut Her Claws

# The Cat Who Cut Her Claws

THERE WAS once a most beautiful cat called Smoky. She was the colour of blue-grey smoke, and had long thick fur and lovely golden eyes. Everybody thought she was wonderful.

Smoky thought herself wonderful too. When she sat washing herself on the wall she loved to see people looking up at her and saying, 'Oh! Look at that marvellous cat!'

The other cats thought she was lovely too, but they didn't tell her so, because they thought that she was vain enough already.

'You know,' said Cinders, the black cat, 'Smoky is

really rather foolish. She can't even catch a mouse!'

Now Smoky was just the other side of the wall, and she heard what Cinders said. She jumped up on to the wall and spat at Cinders in a very rude way.

'I am very clever indeed!' she said. '*You* may not think so – but the two-legged people do. They are always telling me so! Why, I can even rattle at a door handle to tell people I want to get into a room.'

'Really!' said Tabby, a grey-striped little cat. 'Well, I don't do that, Smoky – *I* just jump in at the window!'

The cats laughed, and Smoky jumped down in a temper. She went into her house and looked for her mistress, who always made a great fuss of her. She was in her bedroom, dressing herself ready to go out.

'Hallo, Smoky darling!' she said. 'What a beauty you are! But what have you been doing to your lovely fur? You have dust on it!'

Smoky's mistress took a little brush that she kept specially for the cat and brushed her fur well. Smoky purred. Ah, what did other cats know about having their fur brushed? What other cat had a basket with a silk cushion in it? What other cat had a white china bowl with her name on as Smoky had?

Smoky sat and looked at her mistress. She saw her wash her hands and face. *I do that too*, thought Smoky, *but my tongue and paws are my soap and sponge!*

Then her mistress brushed her hair. *My hair has been brushed too*, thought Smoky proudly. *I am really much more like a two-legged creature than a cat!*

Her mistress sprayed herself with a sweet-smelling scent. Smoky sniffed the smell and liked it. She stood up and mewed to her mistress.

'What! You want some scent too!' said her mistress, laughing. 'Very well! I will spray you with some!'

So Smoky had some scent like her mistress, and she felt so proud that she really couldn't sit still any longer but went prowling up and down the room, purring loudly.

'And now I must do my nails!' said Smoky's

mistress, getting out her little nail scissors and file and tiny bottle of varnish.

*Ah! Nails!* thought Smoky, and came close to see what her mistress was going to do. *Mistress always calls her claws 'nails'. What does she do to them? I must watch.*

Smoky watched her mistress trimming her nails and filing them shorter. She watched her paint them with a little pale pink stuff from the tiny bottle to make them shiny.

'There!' said Smoky's mistress, showing the cat her nails. 'Don't they look nice? They are not horribly sharp and long like *yours*, Smoky! Oh, how I should hate to have cats' claws! Good gracious! Look at the time! I must run or I shall miss my bus.'

She ran downstairs and left Smoky in the bedroom. Smoky looked at the nail scissors and file and tiny bottle. So her nails were horribly sharp and long? Well, why shouldn't she cut them and paint them a pretty pale pink so that they shone like glass?

*I'm washed, I'm brushed, I've got scent on me*, thought

# THE CAT WHO CUT HER CLAWS

Smoky. *And now I don't see why I shouldn't make my claws into nails. I shall* really *be like my mistress then!*

So what do you think that vain cat did? She cut off the sharp points of her eighteen claws. She filed them down neatly. Then she tried to put the shiny varnish on them out of the little bottle. But she upset the bottle and made a great mess on the carpet!

She put out her claws and dipped them all into the spilt varnish. Then she let them dry, and soon they were as shiny as her mistress's had been. How proud Smoky was!

'I must go and show all the other cats,' she said. 'They will certainly think I am clever to have nails instead of claws!'

So off she went and miaowed so loudly that every cat from the gardens around came running at once.

Smoky sat on the ground and looked at the cats with her big golden eyes.

'Look how clever I am!' she said, putting out her short, blunt, shiny claws. 'I have nails instead of claws.

I watched how my mistress did it – and now I am like her. Smell me too – she put some of her scent on me!'

The cats looked at the strange claws in surprise. They turned up their noses at the sweet smell that came from Smoky.

'You are foolish,' said Cinders. 'Very, very foolish. You think you are clever – but you will soon find out how silly you are, and you will be sorry that you have nails instead of claws.'

'You only say that because you are jealous of me,' said Smoky grandly. 'I know that you all wish you had nails instead of claws, but I shan't tell you how to get them. That is my secret!'

'We don't want to know,' said Tabby.

'Listen! A dog!' cried Cinders suddenly.

He was right. In at the gate rushed a big dog, his pink tongue hanging out, his eyes gleaming to see so many cats to chase! 'Woof!' he said and ran towards the little crowd of frightened animals.

Tabby rushed up a tree. Cinders leapt up the fence.

The others ran for their lives, and so did Smoky.

Smoky had such a curious and unusual smell that the dog chose to chase *her*! So down the garden went Smoky, and after her went the dog, barking madly.

Smoky was terrified! She ran and ran and the dog ran too. 'I must jump up a tree!' panted poor Smoky.

So she ran to a tree and tried to claw her way up it. But, alas for Smoky, her claws were now only short blunt nails and she could not dig them into the bark of the tree and hold on as she leapt up. She fell down to the ground and the dog nearly caught her! Off she went again, feeling more afraid than ever. She couldn't even fight the dog, for she had no claws to claw him with! Oh, how could she have been so foolish as to make her fine claws into useless nails!

Goodness knows what would have happened to poor Smoky if Cinders and Tabby hadn't come to her rescue. They knew that she now had no sharp claws and would sooner or later be caught by the dog, so up they ran. One leapt on to the dog's tail and one clawed at his hind legs. The dog turned to snap at the two cats, and that just gave Smoky the chance to jump right over the wall and run home.

She hid behind the sofa, panting and puffing. She felt very silly and very much ashamed.

'I've been so vain and foolish that I nearly got caught by a dog!' she said to herself. 'I shall let my claws grow very, very long! Oh, how I hate the look of them now – silly, useless nails!'

That evening Smoky told Cinders and Tabby how sorry she was for being so silly, and she thanked them for saving her. 'If it hadn't been for your good strong claws, I would be chewed up by that horrid dog by now!' she said. 'Forgive me for being vain and foolish. I see now that I am not at all clever. Please teach me to catch mice when my claws have grown.'

'Very well,' said Cinders. 'Maybe your mistress will like you better still, if you have claws to catch mice with instead of nails to make you vain!'

Cinders was right. Smoky's mistress was delighted

when she began to catch mice. 'I thought you were a silly, beautiful cat without any brains at all!' she said, hugging Smoky. 'But now I see that you are as clever as you are beautiful!'

# The Voice in the Shed

# The Voice in the Shed

THE NEW gardener wasn't at all nice. The children didn't like him a bit. 'He shouts at me,' said Ann. 'Even if I'm only just walking down the path, he shouts at me.'

'And he told me he'd put my wheelbarrow on his bonfire, if I left it out in the garden again,' said John.

'And today he said we weren't to go into the shed any more,' said Peter. 'Why, we've *always* been allowed in the shed, ever since we can remember. It's our shed, not his.'

'I shall tell Daddy I don't like him,' said John.

But Daddy only laughed. 'Old Mr Jacks let you do anything you liked.'

'Mr Jacks was nice,' said Ann. 'I liked him. He gave me strawberry plants for my garden.'

'This new man, Mr Tanner, is a very good gardener,' said Daddy. 'Much better than old Jacks was. Maybe he thinks you children will run over his seedbeds or something. Keep out of his way.'

But they couldn't very well keep out of Mr Tanner's way, because, after all, they had to play in the garden – and, except for Sundays, Mr Tanner was always there, keeping a lookout for them.

He ordered them off whenever he came across them. He grumbled if they dared to pick anything. But he was crossest of all if he caught them in the garden shed.

'You're not to go in there,' he stormed. 'How many times do I have to tell you? I keep my things in there and I'm not having a lot of children messing about with them. You keep out.'

'But we've *always* played in the shed if we wanted to,' said John boldly.

'Well, you won't any more,' said Mr Tanner disagreeably. 'I'll lock it, see?'

He not only locked it, he frightened Ann and Peter very much. He caught them peeping in at the shed window one day and he yelled at them so crossly that they almost fell off the water butt in fright.

'You be careful,' he said. 'I'm going to put someone in there to scare you out! See? You be careful.'

'Who?' asked Ann fearfully.

'Ah, you wait and see,' said Mr Tanner. 'I'll have my Someone there very soon – and won't he chase you when you come messing around!'

Ann and Peter didn't like this idea at all. Who was this horrid Someone? Ann dreamt about it at night and told John. He was the oldest of the three and he laughed.

'It's only something that Mr Tanner has made up to scare you,' he said. 'He hasn't got a Someone.'

But Ann and Peter didn't believe John. They were quite sure that Mr Tanner was horrid enough to keep a strange Someone in their garden shed to scare them away. They didn't go near the shed after that.

'You shouldn't scare my sister and brother like that,' said John boldly to Mr Tanner. 'It's wrong.'

'You get away,' said Mr Tanner in his surly voice. 'I'll do as I like. Pests of children you are. I never did like a place with kids about.'

John went off. He was angry. How dare old Tanner scare Ann and Peter? He went to call on his friend Tom who lived just down the road. He told Tom all about it.

Tom listened. 'Does Mr Tanner have his dinner in that shed?' he asked.

'Yes. Why?' asked John.

'Well, I've got an idea,' said Tom. 'What about *us* putting a Someone in that shed – a Someone who'll scare old Tanner stiff?'

'How can we do that?' asked John in wonder.

284

'Well, listen,' said Tom. 'You know my mother's parrot, don't you? He says all kinds of things in that funny, hollow voice of his. Couldn't we stick him in the shed somewhere and hide him? He'll talk as soon as old Tanner goes in – and what a fright he'll get when he hears a voice and can't see anyone who owns it!'

John was thrilled. 'But what would your mother say if your parrot isn't here at home?' he asked.

'Mother's away for a few days,' said Tom. 'Old Mr Polly, our parrot, won't mind where we put him so long as he has plenty of sunflower seeds to eat. Anyway, we can always go and take him out of the shed when Mr Tanner has gone at five o'clock.'

So that was how old Mr Polly, Tom's parrot, came to be hidden inside the garden shed. He was put there in his big cage, with plenty of food and water. One side of the cage was covered with a sack to hide it.

'Now then you, now then,' remarked Mr Polly in a curious hoarse voice as the boys arranged his cage in the shed. He coughed in a nasty hollow way. 'Fetch a doctor. AtishOOOO!'

He gave such a life-like sneeze that John jumped. Tom giggled. 'It's all right. He's full of silly ways and sayings. Hasn't he got a lovely voice? My word, he'll make Mr Tanner jump!'

The next day Mr Tanner saw John near the garden shed with Peter, and he spoke to them sharply. 'What did I tell you? Clear off – or the Someone in that shed will get you!'

Peter ran off, looking scared.

John spoke up at once. 'You're right, Mr Tanner. There *is* a Someone in the shed. I heard his voice – a deep, hollow kind of voice. I wonder you're not scared too.'

'Aha,' said Mr Tanner, 'what did I say? You be careful of that shed!'

The parrot in the shed coughed solemnly. The sound came out to where Mr Tanner stood with John. He looked a little startled.

'There,' said John, cocking his head on one side. 'Your Someone is coughing. Why don't you give him some cough medicine?'

'It's only the old gardener in the next-door garden,' said Mr Tanner and drove his fork into the ground. 'You clear off.'

Old Mr Polly began to whistle a mournful tune inside the shed.

'Hear that?' said John. 'Your Someone is whistling now. You really *have* got a Someone there, haven't you? Aren't you scared too?'

'I told you to clear off,' said Mr Tanner, looking rather uneasy.

John grinned and went off, very pleased with himself.

Mr Tanner couldn't imagine where the curious noises were coming from that morning. Once he heard a voice – a deep, solemn voice. It certainly sounded as if it came from the shed. Another time he heard a cough, and yet another time a sneeze. Yet, when he went and looked into the shed there was nobody there.

John went to tell Ann and Peter what he and Tom had done. They listened in amazement. Peter laughed. 'I'm glad. Let's go and take our lunch near the shed today if Mother will let us, then we can see what happens.'

So they took a picnic lunch to the back of the shed as soon as Mr Tanner had gone inside to eat *his* lunch!

Mr Tanner opened his lunch packet. He was just about to take up a cheese sandwich when a hollow voice spoke loudly and solemnly.

'There's NO rest for the wicked. Ah me, ah me! Fetch a doctor!'

Mr Tanner was so startled that he dropped his sandwich on the floor. He turned round to see who had spoken, but there was nobody there.

*It must be somebody outside the shed!* Mr Tanner picked up his sandwich and began to eat it.

The voice began again. 'Seesaw, Margery daw, seesaw, sawsee, seesaw, sawsee . . .'

Mr Tanner began to tremble. He dropped his sandwich again.

'Who's there?' he said in a shaky voice. 'Who is it?'

'Here comes a candle to light you to bed, here comes a CHOPPER!' shouted the voice very suddenly, and gave a dreadful squawk that made Mr Tanner leap to his feet in fright, half expecting to see a candle and a chopper coming at him from somewhere.

'Who are you?' cried Mr Tanner, and jumped as John came to the door of the shed. John had heard all this and was thrilled. He looked at the frightened gardener.

'Is that your Someone talking to you?' he asked. 'Why do you look so afraid? It's *your* Someone, isn't it?'

Old Mr Polly took it into his head at that moment to give an imitation of an aeroplane coming down low. He always did this extremely well, and it scared poor old Tanner almost out of his life. It even startled John.

Mr Tanner stumbled over a few pots and fled out

of the door into the bright sunshine. He was trembling all over.

'I can't go in there again,' he told John. 'You fetch out my tools for me. I'm going.'

And when John gave him the few tools that belonged to him off he went, looking very pale.

The children watched him go, feeling pleased.

'His Someone came to life and frightened him!' said John with a grin. 'I'll go and get Tom and we'll carry old Mr Polly back home again. Good Mr Polly – he acted well! My word, did you hear him imitate an aeroplane?'

Mr Polly obligingly did it again. It was wonderful! John pulled the sacking off his cage, and the three children stood and watched the old parrot admiringly.

'What will Daddy say when he hears Mr Tanner has gone?' asked Ann.

Daddy was glad! 'I've heard bad things about that fellow the last day or two!' he said. 'Very bad. He isn't honest, for one thing. I'm glad he's gone. I'll get old

Mr Jacks back again. He's not so good a gardener, but he's absolutely honest and trustworthy.'

'Oh, *good*!' said all the children. 'We do like Mr Jacks.'

And back came old Mr Jacks, beaming all over his face. 'Well, I'm downright pleased to see you all again,' he said. 'I can't think why that fellow Tanner went off as he did. Do you know what he told me?'

'No, what?' asked John.

'He told me not to go into the garden shed!' said old Mr Jacks with a roar of laughter. 'Said there was a voice there that frightened him away. A *voice*! Did you ever hear of such a thing? Is there a voice there, John? What do you say to that?'

'No, there isn't any voice there – not now old Tanner's gone anyway,' said John, and he laughed. 'He scared us by telling us he kept a Someone there, Mr Jacks – but when his Someone grew a voice he didn't like it. He ran away.'

'What tales you tell!' said Mr Jacks, not believing a

word. 'Well, voice or no voice, I'm having my dinner in that shed as usual every day – and, what's more, you can come and share it whenever you like.'

'Thank you!' said all three joyfully. So they often do – but they've none of them heard that voice again! It isn't really very surprising, is it?

# The Tail of Sausages

# The Tail of Sausages

ONCE UPON a time there was a dog who lived next door to a butcher's. This butcher made pork and beef sausages every Friday, and Bingo the dog was so fond of these that he would somehow or other manage to steal a string of them when the butcher was not looking.

His mistress was very cross with him when the butcher came and told her what Bingo did. She had to pay for the sausages, and she scolded Bingo hard.

'You are a little thief!' she said. 'I am ashamed of you, Bingo! You are *not* to take the butcher's sausages any more.'

But on the next Friday, when Bingo saw the strings of sausages lying on the slab in the butcher's shop he quite forgot all his mistress had told him. He crept up when the butcher was not looking, snapped at the string of sausages and quietly ran off with them to his favourite hiding place just under the lilac bush.

It so happened that his mistress was walking down the garden just afterwards – and she heard the sound of munching under the lilac bush. She looked there – and, dear me, when she saw Bingo gobbling *another* string of sausages how upset she was!

'I shall have to pay the butcher again!' she cried. 'You naughty dog! Come here!'

But Bingo wouldn't come. He slipped away the other side of the bush and ran off, licking his lips. Oh, those sausages *were* good!

He didn't see his mistress put on her hat and coat. He didn't see her go out of the gate and turn towards the funny little shop that stood all alone at the end of the village. If he *had* seen her, he might have felt worried for she was going to buy something that would stop him stealing sausages for ever!

Dame Snooty kept the funny little shop. There were big bottles full of interesting powders and great jars of strange-smelling liquids. Dame Snooty was very wise, and she used to go out into the countryside early each morning, collecting rare plants and herbs, which she boiled and made into curious medicines and powders. She had a powder or a medicine for almost everything under the sun, from a little bruise to sunstroke.

Bingo's mistress told her about her naughty little dog, and Dame Snooty shook her silvery head in horror when she heard about all the sausages he stole.

'I can give you a yellow powder for him,' she said. 'I don't quite know how it will work, but it will certainly stop him from stealing sausages any more!'

'Oh, thank you!' said Bingo's mistress. 'I'll take it now.'

Dame Snooty emptied some bright yellow powder into a little blue box and gave it to Bingo's mistress, who paid her a silver sixpence for it.

That night Bingo's mistress put the yellow powder into Bingo's drinking water, and when the little dog came home he was so thirsty that he drank every drop. He thought it tasted a bit funny, but he was so thirsty that it didn't bother him at all.

Nothing happened that night, nor the next day. Nothing happened the day after that either. Bingo felt just the same as usual, but Bingo's mistress was quite sure that when Friday came Bingo would suddenly feel that he wasn't going to steal sausages any more. She thought he would be a good dog and never steal again because of the yellow powder she had given him.

Friday came – and, dear me, when Bingo smelt that lovely sausage smell he just couldn't think of saying no to it.

'I *must* get some of those sausages!' he woofed to

himself. 'I don't care what happens. I *must* have some!'

So he played his usual trick of waiting until the butcher's back was turned and then running off with a long string of brown sausages! He sat down in a quiet corner to eat them, and when he had gobbled up every single one of them he lay down to sleep.

When he awoke he sat up and yawned. Then off he ran to go home – but something funny seemed to be behind him. He looked round – and whatever do you think had happened? Why, his tail had changed into a long string of brown sausages!

Yes! He had no longer got his little stump of a wagging tail. It had gone, and instead he had this long string of sausages growing on to him. Bingo was astonished. At first he thought someone had tied them on to him, so he bit them, meaning to eat them.

But he hurt himself when he bit – for the sausages were his tail now, and it was just as if he had bitten his tail! He yelped with pain and sat down to look at the sausages. What a very peculiar thing – they certainly were growing on him! However could it have happened?

Bingo didn't know what to do. He thought he had better go home to his mistress and see what she said. So off he trotted.

But he had forgotten that he might meet other dogs and cats too. As soon as they smelt his sausage tail, they ran after him in delight. Sausages! Sausages! The news went round and soon twenty-two dogs and sixteen cats were all round Bingo, trying their hardest to eat his sausage tail!

It hurt him dreadfully every time they bit him. They wouldn't leave him. They kept snapping and biting at his strange tail till he yelped with fright. At last he got home and ran whining to his mistress.

But when *she* saw his tail she laughed! Yes, she laughed and laughed – for she saw what that yellow powder had done, and she thought it was a very good punishment for Bingo.

'Ah, you see, Bingo,' she said, 'you are so fond of

sausages that your tail has grown into a string of them. Now what will you do? You had better stop eating sausages altogether, or you might find that you had turned into a great big sausage yourself. Let your tail be a warning to you!'

Bingo was upset and unhappy. He crept into his kennel with his strange tail and lay down, trying to hide it. He wouldn't come out at all. He lay there all the week, eating just a few biscuits and drinking a little water, but nothing else. When Friday came he smelt the sausages at the butcher's next door. He was hungry, but he didn't stir out of his kennel to go and steal those sausages.

No, he didn't want to see or taste sausages in his life again. He had lived with a tail of sausages all the week, and he hated them.

Bingo crept out of his kennel to have a drink of water, keeping a good lookout for any dog or cat that might be near. He was so afraid they would smell his sausage tail and come to eat it. He looked round at it – and to his great delight it was shorter! Instead of being six sausages long, it was only five. One of the sausages had disappeared!

*Perhaps if I am a good, obedient dog and never steal again, my tail will disappear*, thought Bingo. So he went to his mistress and told her he had made up his mind never to be naughty again. As he told her that his tail became shorter still. Another sausage was gone!

Well, before another week had passed Bingo's sausage tail had disappeared, and his own stumpy tail had grown instead. How pleased he was! How he wagged it to make sure it was all right! He was delighted.

And now he never goes near the butcher's shop on Fridays, and the butcher thinks he is a good little dog and often gives him a bone to gnaw. Sometimes – just sometimes – he forgets his promise to be good, and then his mistress looks at him and shakes her head.

'Sausages, Bingo,' she says. 'Remember the sausages!'

Then Bingo remembers and you should see how his ears and tail droop in shame!

# The Next-Door Cat

# The Next-Door Cat

'THERE'S THAT lovely ginger cat who lives next door,' said Mummy. 'He's in our garden, look. Go and stroke him, Janie – he's a real pet.'

'I don't like him,' said Janie. 'He's a horrid, unkind cat. He caught a blackbird the other day, and he scratched me when I took it away from him.'

'Well, darling, it's a cat's nature to catch birds – and mice and rats,' said Mummy. 'He can't help himself.'

'If *I* was a cat, I'd feel very muddled when my mistress *praised* me for catching mice but *blamed* me for catching birds,' said Harry. 'I wouldn't know *what* to think!'

'I don't care what you say. I still don't like that cat Ginger,' said Janie. 'I shall chase him away.'

'No, don't,' said Mummy. 'He wouldn't understand. He would think you were a nasty, unkind little girl – and you aren't.'

'Let's go and fly our kite,' said Harry, getting up. 'It's a lovely windy day. You get the string, Janie, and I'll get the kite. I bet that cat will run away as soon as he sees our kite bobbing in the air. You won't have to chase him!'

The two children were soon out in the garden with their kite. It wasn't very big, but it was a very nice one. Uncle Fred had given it to them when he had come to see Mummy.

Ginger the cat ran to the wall when he saw the two children. He liked Harry but he was afraid of Janie because sometimes she chased him and shouted at him. She still felt cross because of the blackbird he had caught. Ginger leapt up on to the wall and lay there, watching what the children were doing.

Janie got in a muddle with the string, so Harry put the kite down on the ground and went to help her. The wind jiggled the kite and it flapped a little, moving along over the grass. Ginger watched it with great interest. Was it alive? Why did it jiggle and flap like that? He longed to jump down and catch it!

The kite wriggled and shook when another gust of wind came, and Ginger crouched, ready to pounce on it if it came any nearer the wall. What fun to catch it! But he didn't dare to leap down in case Janie chased him away.

At last the muddled, tangled string was undone, and then the children began to fly the kite. Harry picked it up from the grass and threw it into the wind. The breeze caught it and played with it, making it flap and fling itself up and down in the air.

Ginger watched it, amazed. So this thing could fly! Was it a kind of bird? He was very interested indeed and never took his eye off the kite.

Suddenly the kite flew high into the air, and Ginger

PET STORIES

stood up eagerly. Yes, it *must* be a bird! A bird that belonged to the two children. A tame bird on a string.

Just as Harry was flying the kite beautifully, and almost all the string had run out, Mummy called him. 'Harry! Come and get these hot buns straight out of the oven; there's one for each of you.'

'Hold the kite, Janie,' said Harry, and pushed the piece of wood on which the string was wound into Janie's hand. She was delighted. Now *she* could fly the kite – and she would fly it higher than Harry! She pulled and jerked at the kite high up in the air and it didn't like it. Then the wind suddenly dropped a little, and the kite took a swooping leap downwards – and fell on to the roof next door!

There it stuck. Janie pulled and pulled at the string, but the kite wouldn't move. Then she pulled so hard that the string broke with a snap! She stared in horror.

'Oh! Harry *will* be cross. We'll never be able to get the kite down from there. Oh, wind, do blow it down!'

But although the wind did blow with all its might,

310

it wouldn't move the kite. It just jiggled and flapped, but stayed where it was, stuck on the roof.

Ginger the cat was still very interested. So that funny big bird had flown on to the roof, had it, just as the starlings did when he ran after them! The starlings sat up on the roof and spluttered and gurgled at him when he chased them away – and now it seemed to him as if the kite was laughing at poor Janie! Ginger turned himself right round and gazed up at it. It was on his own roof, and he wondered if it was ever going to fly off.

Janie ran indoors, crying, 'Harry! The string broke and the kite's stuck on the roof next door ever so high. Oh, Harry!'

As soon as Janie had run indoors, Ginger leapt down into his own garden and ran to his house. Up the side of it, nailed to the wall, was a trellis on which climbing roses grew. Ginger had often climbed up to frighten the cheeky chaffinch who called him rude names from the top.

Up he went, paw over paw. Then he leapt on to a small roof and from there he climbed up to the top roof of all, clinging to the thick ivy stems that grew up the wall. He climbed across the gutter and then sat on the tiles to see where that strange flapping bird had got to that Jane had been flying.

Ah, there it was! It seemed to be caught and couldn't fly. Its string was entangled in a loose tile. Perhaps he could catch it. But was it good to eat? Ginger didn't think so. He took a cautious step towards it, and then went hurriedly back as the wind blew and made the kite jiggle and shake.

*It's afraid of me*, thought Ginger and on he went again. He sat down close beside it. It didn't bite him, or peck him as the blackbird had done. *Was* it a bird? Perhaps it wasn't, even though it could fly so well.

Ginger put out a paw and tapped the kite gently. It jiggled a little, but that was all. He put out his paw once more. He wanted this funny thing to fly again.

Why wouldn't it? Perhaps if he scrabbled at it, it would come loose and fly off. Then he could jump down and chase it.

Just then Harry and Janie came out into the garden, Harry was still cross about his kite. He stared up then gave a shout.

'Look, Ginger's up there! Oh, Janie, I do believe he's trying to set the kite free. Look at him patting and pushing it! Good old Ginger!'

Janie was astonished. It really did look as if Ginger was trying to free the kite, and then, with a sudden scratch of his paw, the string loosened – and the kite rose into the air!

'*Whoo-oo-oo!*' said the wind in delight, and blew it high in the air. Then down it flew into Harry's garden, flapping and swinging here and there, trailing its string behind it. And after it raced Ginger – down to the small roof, on to the ground, up on the wall again and into Harry's garden. The kite had just landed there, and Ginger leapt on it in delight. He had caught it, whatever it was! How proud he was!

'Clever cat!' said Harry, pleased to have his kite again. 'Kind cat! Wonderful cat! You got the kite down and now you've caught it for us so that it cannot blow away till we've got hold of the string again. Janie, isn't he a *good* cat?'

Janie ran to Ginger, and at first he thought she was going to chase him away as usual. But she didn't. She stroked him and fussed him and petted him. 'Dear Ginger! Good Ginger! Oh, Harry – he got the kite down, isn't he CLEVER?'

'Very,' said Harry, winding up the string. 'But *you're* not clever, Janie. I shan't let you fly the kite any more!'

'Well, I don't care!' said Janie, and picked up Ginger. 'I'll go indoors and give Ginger the creamiest drink of milk he's ever had. I don't hate him any more. I love him!'

So now Ginger is a very spoilt cat. As Janie's mother says he has *two* homes – one with Janie, and one next door!

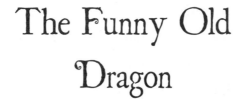

# The Funny Old Dragon

# The Funny Old Dragon

ONE WINTRY morning James had the biggest surprise of his life! He was going across the field path on a misty day when he heard something snorting in the field over the hedge.

'I wonder what it is,' he said, and he peeped to see. And, goodness gracious me, in the next field was a dragon! Yes, a dragon, just like you see in a storybook, with a long spiky tail and four clawed feet!

James was so astonished that he stared and stared and stared.

The dragon saw him and nodded to him. 'Good day,' he said in a mournful voice. 'I'm looking for work. Can you tell me of any?'

'Well,' said James, still more surprised to hear the dragon's strange, husky voice. 'I'm afraid I don't know of any work a dragon can do. How did you come here? I didn't know there were any dragons at all nowadays.'

'There shouldn't be really,' said the dragon. 'But somehow I grew, though I know I'm dreadfully out of date and useless. Nobody wants a dragon nowadays, not even to fight with. So I left the place where I lived and came out to look for work. I'm very unhappy.'

James squeezed through the hedge. He was sorry for the dragon who had very large soft brown eyes. He took a good look at him.

'Well, I should think you'd better keep yourself hidden,' he said. 'It's not likely anyone would be frightened of you nowadays, but you might be caught and put into the zoo in a great big cage, like the lions and tigers and bears – and you might not like that!'

'Oh, no, I shouldn't!' said the dragon in alarm. 'Couldn't you take me home with you and let me be your pet? I've a very sweet, loving nature really.'

'No, I don't think my mother would like a dragon on the rug in front of the fire,' said James. 'In fact, I'm sure she wouldn't. And Daddy would say you smelt.'

'Smelt!' said the dragon, offended. 'Do I smell? What do I smell of?'

'You smell of smoke,' said James, sniffing.

'Ah, that's because I can breathe out fire and smoke just like the old dragons could in the fairy tales!' said the dragon. 'Watch!'

James watched. The dragon breathed out a lot of smoke from his nose and mouth, and a long red flame spurted out too. The dragon looked proudly at James.

'What do you think of that?' he said. 'A good trick, isn't it?'

'My goodness!' said James. 'You'd be useful to Daddy when he lights bonfires! A puff of your flame and smoke and any bonfire would go well! I wish *I* could do that!'

'Listen, boy!' said the dragon excitedly. 'Couldn't I help with people's bonfires? I could hide in a chimney in the daytime somewhere, and then my breath coming out at the top would look like chimney smoke – but at night I could creep out and go all around puffing at people's bonfires and making them burn well. I should love that. That would be a real good piece of work for me to do!'

'Well, if I let you do that, will you teach me how to breathe out fire and smoke just like you do?' asked James longingly.

'Of course!' said the dragon.

So they shook hands solemnly, and James managed to take the dragon to his house by the side door, get him into the study and stuff him up the chimney without anyone seeing.

The dragon was long, but not fat, so he was quite all right in the chimney. His breath shot out at the top, and no one thought it was anything else but ordinary chimney smoke.

That night James gave him a tug and he slid neatly down and slipped out into the garden. He went to the bonfire that James's daddy had tried to light. There had been a shower of rain and the bonfire was almost out.

'*Puff! Fffffffff! Puff!*' went the dragon busily, blowing out smoke and flames. The bonfire flared up at once and the rubbish began to burn merrily. The dragon laughed and so did James. This was fun!

'Where's the next bonfire?' asked the dragon. 'I don't feel useless and out of date any more, James. I *am* enjoying myself!'

Well, the old dragon got everybody's bonfire burning very well indeed, and James knew that all the gardeners and daddies would be simply delighted the next day. And he would be the only one that knew the secret! James felt rather grand.

'Teach me how to breathe fire and smoke, please,

Dragon,' he said. 'You promised you would.'

So the dragon gave him his first lesson. My goodness, it was most exciting, I can tell you! James was able to breathe out just a little bit of blue smoke at the end of his first lesson.

'*Hoo!*' said James. 'Won't I make the boys stare at school! My word, no one will dare to be rude to me when I can breathe out fire and smoke! I *shall* have fun!'

The dragon went back to his chimney after that and James crept into bed.

Every night they went out together, and soon they were very fond of one another indeed. The dragon was the kindest-hearted creature, very fond of a joke, and James did wish he could build him a large kennel and have him for a pet. But somehow he felt sure people wouldn't like it.

'I'm very happy now,' the dragon told James. 'I have good work to do – and I have a friend. That is all I want. Be sure to let me know, dear James, whenever any of your friends want their bonfires kept burning in the night, and you may be sure I will go and do what I can for them.'

So if your daddy can't get his bonfire to burn well, send me a card for James and I'm sure he'll arrange things for you. And *if* you meet a boy who can breathe fire and smoke out of his mouth and nose, you'll know who he is – it will be James, the only boy in the kingdom who keeps a dragon up the chimney!

# Acknowledgements

All efforts have been made to seek necessary permissions.

The stories in this publication first appeared in the following publications:

'The Mysterious Thief' first appeared in *Enid Blyton's Sunny Stories*, No. 64, 1938.

'The Rabbit With a Gold Tail' first appeared in *The Teachers World*, No. 907, 1922.

'The Glittering Diamond' first appeared as 'Untitled' in *The Teachers World*, No. 1468, 1931.

'Twelve Silver Cups' first appeared in *Enid Blyton's Sunny Stories*, No. 146, 1939.

'Granny's Kittens' first appeared in *Enid Blyton's Sunny Stories*, No. 433, 1948.

'Catch Him Quick' first appeared as 'Catch Him Quick!' in *Enid Blyton's Sunny Stories*, No. 390, 1946.

'Pinkity's Party Frock' first appeared in *Enid Blyton's Sunny Stories*, No. 91, 1938.

'A Tale of Sooty and Snowy' first appeared in *Enid Blyton's Sunny Stories*, No. 509, 1951.

'Rover's Hide-and-Seek' first appeared in *Sunny Stories for Little Folks*, No. 236, 1936.

'Snubby's Tail' first appeared in *Sunny Stories for Little Folks*, No. 247, 1936.

'The Lucky Jackdaw' first appeared in *Sunny Stories for Little Folks*, No. 102, 1930.

'The Tale of Kimmy-Cat' first appeared in *Sunny Stories for Little Folks*, No. 95, 1930.

'The Tale of the Tadpoles' first appeared in *Sunday Mail*, No. 1903, 1945.

'Master Prickly' first appeared in *The Enid Blyton Nature Readers*, No. 34, published by Macmillan in 1955.

'The Puppy and the Pixie' first appeared in *Sunny Stories for Little Folks*, No. 194, 1934.

'Surprise for Mother and Susan' first appeared as 'A Surprise for Mother and Susan' in *Enid Blyton's Sunny Stories*, No. 372, 1946.

'Mr Twiddle and His Wife's Hat' first appeared in *Enid Blyton's Sunny Stories*, No. 194, 1940.

'The Lost Slippers' first appeared in *Enid Blyton's Sunny Stories*, No. 7, 1937.

'Robina's Robins' first appeared in *Enid Blyton's Magazine*, No. 21, Vol. 5, 1957.

'The Tale of a Goldfish' first appeared in *The Enid Blyton Nature Readers*, No. 33, published by Macmillan in 1955.

'The New Little Milkman' first appeared in *Enid Blyton's Sunny Stories*, No. 261, 1942.

'Go Away, Black Cat!' first appeared in *Enid Blyton's Sunny Stories*, No. 179, 1940.

'Pippitty's Pet Canary' first appeared in *Sunny Stories for Little Folks*, No. 108, 1930.

'The Foolish Guinea Pig' first appeared in *Enid Blyton's Sunny Stories*, No. 10, 1937.

'The Dog Without a Collar' first appeared in *Sunny Stories for Little Folks*, No. 161, 1933.

'The Cat Who Cut Her Claws' first appeared in *Enid Blyton's Sunny Stories*, No. 188, 1940.

'The Voice in the Shed' first appeared in *Enid Blyton's Sunny Stories*, No. 475, 1950.

'The Tail of Sausages' first appeared in *Sunny Stories for Little Folks*, No. 177, 1933.

'The Next-Door Cat' first appeared in *Enid Blyton's Magazine*, No. 21, Vol. 5, 1957.

'The Funny Old Dragon' first appeared in *Enid Blyton's Sunny Stories*, No. 104, 1939.

# Enid Blyton®

## STORIES OF

# ROTTEN RASCALS

**30 stories**

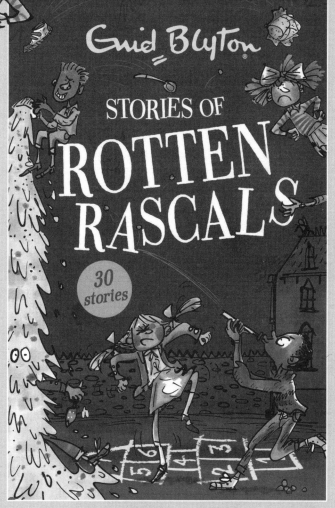

*Meet some hair-raisingly horrid children in these classic stories from the world's best-loved storyteller!*

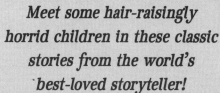

# Enid Blyton

is one of the most popular children's authors of all time. Her books have sold over 500 million copies and have been translated into other languages more often than any other children's author.

Enid Blyton adored writing for children. She wrote over 700 books and about 2,000 short stories. *The Famous Five* books, now 75 years old, are her most popular. She is also the author of other favourites including *The Secret Seven*, *The Magic Faraway Tree*, *Malory Towers* and *Noddy*.

Born in London in 1897, Enid lived much of her life in Buckinghamshire and loved dogs, gardening and the countryside. She was very knowledgeable about trees, flowers, birds and animals.

Dorset – where some of the Famous Five's adventures are set – was a favourite place of hers too.

Enid Blyton's stories are read and loved by millions of children (and grown-ups) all over the world. Visit enidblyton.co.uk to discover more.